Filthy Ruck

Ruck Boys
Book 1

Maggie Alabaster

Trigger Warnings

This book contains:
- Stripping
- Prostitution
- Drugging
- Consensual non-consent/dubious consent
- Possessive, obsessive men

Chapter One

Chelsea

My BLACK STILETTOS CLICKED ON THE HARD surface of the stage. Music blared, all but drowning out the clinking of glasses and the whistles accompanying my entrance.

I looked out across the eager audience of men. Some regulars, others not. They jostled to get closer, spilling drinks on the floor at their feet. The smell of stale beer and Bundy rum warred with testosterone and sweat.

I scanned the crowd, my gaze falling on one face before sliding away. Keeping the flicker of recognition from my expression. They came here to see, not to be seen.

Still, I couldn't keep from looking back at him.

Eyes focused on that one face in the centre of the audience. His indifference a challenge of sorts.

I did love a challenge.

I kept my attention on him. This show was all for him. No one existed in the whole room but us. My smile was all for him. My performance.

My body.

I gripped the pole with two hands and swung around it, letting momentum carry me around a couple of times.

I locked my focus back on the guy in the audience, pulled myself up higher and wrapped my legs around the pole. It was him I wanted to wrap my legs around. His firm torso I wanted to climb, not the cold metal under my hands.

Holding on with my thighs, I leaned back, my arms stretched out behind me. Right on cue, my dress slid down my body, all the way to my chest. Still gripping the pole with my legs, I undid the ties at the front of my dress and let it fall to the stage like it was pooling at his feet.

The audience cheered and whistled.

Someone shouted, "Get the rest of it off!"

A surge of power and adrenaline coursed through me. It took strength and skill to do what I just did. Holding onto a rotating pole while stripping down to my underwear. Making the audience respond to me, to my body. They thought they were here for one thing—to see me take my clothes off. This was so much more than that. They were the moths and I was the flame, burning bright. Enticing.

I spun around the pole a couple more times before grabbing hold with my hands again and pretending to dry hump the metal. That always got a response.

"Fuck me, baby!" an older guy shouted out.

"Show us your tits!" shouted another.

Zero points for originality.

"It's my last night of freedom, how about you make it memorable?" called out another.

I could and I would.

I climbed up the pole and twisted around so my back was to the audience. I teased them by sliding my hands up and down my skin, then unhooking my bra.

Oh so slowly, I let the straps slide down my arms, to my wrists. I pinched the black lace between my thumb and forefinger of one hand and brandished the garment over my head. A couple of times, I twirled it around beside my head, like I might throw it out into the crowd. With a flourish, I threw it toward the door leading to backstage.

Teasing was one thing, throwing away a perfectly good bra was another. Not to mention Divina, the owner of Flirts, would be pissed if I threw my costume into the crowd and caused the audience to lunge and fight to claim it. As if someone having possession of my garment meant they had possession of me.

I glanced at the audience over my shoulder, taunting them for a couple of minutes before I turned back around.

The guy in the middle of the crowd licked his lips. The first indication I'd broken through his facade. I glanced down to the front of his dark jeans. The telltale bulge in the front spoke louder than the growing desire in his eyes.

I didn't need to look at the rest of the audience; they all were hard. That was what they came here for. To tell themselves I was getting naked for them, to be turned on by it.

They leered at my bare breasts, aching to touch them. I ran my hands up my stomach and over them, pinching my nipples, my eyes half-closed.

I liked turning them on. Being appreciated. Wanted. Needed.

I'd worked hard to sculpt my body, to look the way I did. It didn't hurt that I was blessed with perfect breasts. Why not show them off?

"Let me touch them!" A guy who couldn't have been more than about twenty placed his hands on the stage near my feet and started to climb up. The bouncers were there immediately, pulling him off and hauling him towards the door. Divina was tight with money, but she looked after her dancers. No one would touch us without our permission. Not for lack of trying. There was at least one every night.

The guy in the middle of the audience smirked as the younger man was tossed out. I couldn't make out the colour of his eyes, but he locked them on me and nodded, giving me permission to continue.

I gave him a dazzling smile in return.

I spun around the pole a few more times before holding on with my hands and spreading my legs wide, straight out to either side. As I turned slowly, the audience would get an eyeful of the gusset of my G string.

The shouting continued, the whistling amped up double.

I slid around the pole like a serpent before hooking my thumb around the waistband of my G-string. I pushed one side down a little, then the other side. Only a centimetre or so at first.

Stepping away from the pole, I turned my back on the audience and leaned over to look at them between my legs, giving them a good look of my perfectly rounded ass.

Mr Front Row's eyes were still on me. I didn't think he'd blinked since I stepped foot on stage. With any luck, he had the tips to back it up. I could use a few extra dollars right now.

I straightened up and turned around, my eyes right on his face. I hooked the tips of my fingers into the top of my panties and pushed them down. I stopped for a moment to give him a secret smile. I was getting naked just for him. He and I were alone in the room. My body was all for him.

His visible swallow was all for me.

My panties dropped to the top of my stilettos. I raised one foot, then the other, stepping out of the black lace.

I licked my lips slowly and dropped into a crouch, letting him get an eyeful of my pussy.

He glanced down, eyebrow jerking up at the twinkle of my clit piercing before he looked back at my face.

I'd seen that exact look on the face of so many of

my customers, but somehow it was more pronounced on his. Hunger. Need.

If I let him, he'd claim me right there on the stage in front of everyone. Make me his.

I didn't mind an audience, but Divina would have a coronary on the spot if we fucked on stage. The stage was for stripping. Teasing. The appetiser.

I rose to my feet, did another couple of turns on the pole before I headed backstage. Not before I stopped to blow the audience a kiss. And give Mr Front Row another lingering look.

"Girl, you were on fire tonight." India Hartman-Green gave me a hug before stepping back to let me pull off my stilettos. The youngest of six children, she was outgoing, always smiling. She stripped for the pure fun of it, and because she was good at it. With golden blonde hair and striking blue eyes, she was always a favourite with the customers. Always laughing and flirting and having a good time. There wasn't a person at the club who didn't adore her, especially me. Her joy in life was infectious.

"You think so?" I asked. "I feel like I need to add something else to my act."

"You don't need to add a thing." She patted my shoulder. "You're perfect just the way you are. Don't overthink it, just enjoy yourself."

"I can't help overthinking it," I said dryly. "It's what I do. Chelsea Miller, overthinker."

India giggled. "You're too cute. And so fucking hot. You had those guys out there drooling for you. You'll make a shit ton extra tonight." She winked.

"Just warming them up for the main event," I said. I pulled on clean underwear and a dress that was low-cut in the front and fell to mid thigh.

"Honey, we're *all* the main event." She smiled and stepped out towards the stage, confidence oozing from every pore.

I fixed my hair and make-up and headed out to the bar. Flirts was a big place, with the stage and one bar at one end, and another bar with a quieter lounge at the other. It was to the quieter section I went, moving around the tables and smiling at the customers.

"Nice work tonight," Gary, one of the bouncers, said as he shouldered his way past several customers. He was about seven feet tall and almost as wide, but he wouldn't hurt anyone who didn't provoke him or make trouble with one of the dancers. For someone who had seen my pussy more than most other guys, he was always respectful.

All pussies looked alike after a while, I supposed.

"Thanks," I replied. "You too. Thanks for getting rid of that guy before he became a problem."

Gary shrugged. "All part of the service." He nodded before making his way back to the stage area.

"Hey." A presence loomed beside my right elbow a moment before he spoke.

Almost as big as Gary, his grey-eyed gaze penetrated right into me. Like he'd seen more than my naked body. Mr Front Row made no attempt to touch me. Not yet anyway.

"Hey." I stopped and smiled. Not the plastic smile I usually gave people who approached me here in the club. This one was a little warmer, a little more genuine. Why? Because I sensed he'd see right through that façade. Being facetious wouldn't get me any more money.

"Buy you a drink?" He gestured towards the bar.

"Sure." I stepped over beside him and ordered a house special. Cola on the rocks, no alcohol. I didn't drink on the job. Either of them. Getting drunk here was too dangerous and Divina hated us getting messy. A strip club wasn't a place to let my guard down, not even with the threat of Gary looming over customers.

He ordered a light beer and leaned his elbow on the bar. "I'm guessing Sparkle isn't your real name."

I laughed and took a sip of my drink. "What makes you think that? Don't I look like a Sparkle?" I patted my hair and looked coy.

He snorted. "Fuck no. Unless that's your real name." He clearly didn't believe that for a moment.

"It's not," I admitted. "I didn't even choose it for myself." It was Divina's idea. Of course it was. Who else would come up with a stage name like that?

"What would you choose?" He looked at me over the rim of his glass and raised his eyebrows questioningly.

"I have no idea," I said. "What would you choose for me?" I cocked my head at him. I'd played this game before, but I was curious what someone like him would come up with.

He looked thoughtful. "A cat name. Leopard or Panther. Something smooth and sexy."

That was a better suggestion than the usual 'Hot Tits', or 'Wet Pussy.' Some guys had no imagination.

"I like that," I said. "Panther would have worked. All in black. Leather pants and a black leather bra."

He adjusted his pants. "Panther it is. I'm Storm. Storm Keller. Yes, that's my real name." He offered me his hand.

I shook it. "It suits you. Your eyes are the colour of storm clouds." Almost as dangerous. Something swirled in those depths. Something a girl could get caught up in too easily, if she wasn't careful.

"Yours are the colour of the sky in the middle of winter," he said, looking into mine, appraising me. "Panther with pretty blue eyes."

"Sparkle!" a new voice said from the other side of me. "How much for a blowjob?"

I turned as a handful of fifty dollar notes were pushed in the direction of my chest. They were accompanied by an eager looking customer with desperate eyes.

I was taken aback. Not because I wasn't used to exactly this scenario, but because I had, for a few moments, been caught up in the conversation with Storm.

"Come on, slut," the new guy insisted. "That's what you're here for. You show us your pussy and I fuck your mouth. Right here works for me." He undid the front of his jeans and pushed them down far enough for his small erection to spring free.

"The lady is occupied," Storm said, his voice as dark as the clouds in his eyes. "She's with me." He draped an arm over my shoulders, the tips of his fingers barely touching my upper arm. Possessive, but with a hint of respect.

"Fuck off." The asshole was persistent. "I'm

paying good money for this. She can suck me off and then you can fuck her brains out for all I care. Come on, bitch. On your knees."

"Like he said, I'm occupied," I said coolly.

I looked over to Storm and smiled. "There's a private room we can use, big boy." I slipped out from under his arm, took his hand and led him away from the customer who gaped and swore after us.

Chapter Two

Chelsea

I closed the door behind me and Storm and leaned against it for a moment.

"Thanks. Guys like that really—" I shook my head.

"Need to fuck all the way off," Storm rumbled. He looked tempted to step back outside and acquaint the dickhead with his fist.

"Yeah." I punctuated that with a half-laugh. It was nothing I couldn't handle, but I appreciated him stepping in. Most guys didn't. Some of them pretended not to see, and others would have egged the pushy prick on. Usually, only the bouncers stepped in if the dancers couldn't take care of them-selves. Which, for the most part, we could.

Inside Flirts anyway.

Storm shrugged. "I don't like dickheads. Just because you take your clothes off, doesn't mean you want to go any further." He flopped down in a chair in the corner of the room and crossed his legs.

"It doesn't mean I don't either." I pushed myself off the door and sashayed toward him. "If I wasn't talking to you, and if that guy wasn't so pushy, he might have got his blowjob."

Like India enjoyed dancing, I enjoyed sex. I lost count of the amount of times I'd done it for money. Was I ashamed of it? Not for a moment. I gave pleasure and got money in return. That was a win-win as far as I was concerned.

A flash of surprise crossed Storm's face and his eyes darkened further. "So when you suggested we come here alone..."

I smiled and straddled his thighs. "I owe you one for the expression on that guy's face. He looked like he wasn't used to being told no."

Storm placed his large hands on my hips. "Guys like that never are. They like to take whatever they can get, whether it's freely offered or not. That's why they come to places like this. So they can feel powerful. Or some shit."

"Is that why you came here?" I lightly placed my hands on his chest. Under my palms was hard muscle, threatening to break out of his black Dusk Bay Smashers T-shirt. "To feel powerful?"

He chuckled. "Sweetheart, I don't need to come to a club to feel powerful. I was just here with a bunch of other guys."

"Please say you weren't here with blowjob guy." I grimaced.

"If I knew him, I would have taken him outside and punched the crap out of him" He squeezed my hips. "Is this where I pull out my money? You know, you don't have to do anything you don't want to."

It was my turn to snort. "I know that. There's a panic button under this seat if you get out of control. And a card reader on the table." I jerked my head towards it.

He leaned forward to ease his wallet out of his back pocket and slid out his card. A wave in front of the card reader and a tap on the number keys, and he turned the machine to show me the screen.

My eyes widened. "That's enough for a week."

"A whole week with Panther, hmmm?" He pressed enter.

"I don't have a week." I made to grab the machine and cancel the transaction.

"Then we better make the best of the time we have," he said. He put the card reader out of my reach and raised his hands. "What happens next?"

"You paid all that money, you tell me," I said. For that much, not a whole lot was off the table. "What's your wildest fantasy?"

"My wildest, hmmm?" He cocked his head. "This. Watching a beautiful woman get naked in front of a room full of people, and then taking her somewhere private to be fucked. Knowing all those guys will be jealous of me. Knowing they've all seen your pussy, but I'm the one who's going to get off here." He made no attempt to hide the possessive flavour to his tone. If anything, he was embracing it.

I stood up on either side of his thighs, just high enough to grip the hem of my dress and pull it up and over my head. "Then I better make it worth your while."

"I know you will. Strip for me, Panther." He laced his hands and placed them behind his head.

A smile on the corners of his lips, he sat back and nodded. Once again giving me his permission. And showing his intention to enjoy every second of watching me take my clothes off just for him. Knowing he was the only one who'd see my body this time.

Everything I did right now was all for him and no one else.

I stepped back, my heels clicking on the floor. My eyes on his, I unhooked my bra, and for the second time that evening slid it down my arms and let it drop to the floor.

I turned my back and shimmied out of my panties before placing them aside.

"Sit down in the chair opposite me," he said. "I want to see you touch yourself."

It wasn't the first time I'd received that request. Some guys liked to watch me slide my fingers around my clit. Some liked to know what got me off, so they could do it too. Others wanted to enjoy the show.

So I always gave them one.

I was good at this and I knew it. Getting guys going, making them harder than steel.

I loved every moment of it.

I sat down and opened my knees, giving him a good view of my pussy. I traced circles around my clit with my fingertips before sliding a finger inside myself. With my other hand, I rubbed and pinched my nipple.

Storm opened the front of his jeans and wrapped his hand around his thick erection. He was big. Huge. Enough to make my mouth water.

Slowly, like he was the one being paid for it, he slid his hand up and down his cock, rolling his hips as he matched the rhythm of my own strokes.

Watching him touching himself awakened an almost feral arousal in me. A hungry, burning need. How would his cock feel inside me? He was so big, I'd be full to the brim.

Yes please. I'd take every last centimetre of him all the way inside me.

"Come for me, Panther," he said, his voice deep and low. "I want to see you come."

I half-closed my eyes and rubbed more firmly, driving myself closer and closer.

"Tell me," he insisted.

"I'm... I'm coming," I said breathlessly.

"Don't fake it," he said. "I want to see you come for real."

"I never...fake it," I panted. I'd never seen the point. If I, or my partner, knew how to touch me, then I'd come. If not, they'd learn. I was better at stroking cocks than I was at stroking egos. I saved that for my other job.

I groaned, long and low, before I came, my release making my hand wetter. The world around me went dark. I shattered into a thousand pieces. It wasn't a mind blowing orgasm, just a soft peak of pleasure that took the edge off my tension. I could never give myself what a partner could give to me. Not even with the best vibrator known to humankind. Nothing could get me off like a man's hand or tongue, or cock.

"Fuck... Yeah." He jerked hard on his cock until it exploded, cum squirting out the tip, over his hand and the front of the chair. He stroked himself a few more times before flopping back and taking a deep breath.

After a few moments of silence, he said, "I liked watching you come."

"I liked watching you come too," I said, slightly confused. He hadn't touched me and made no move to do so now.

Instead, he wiped his hand on his shirt and did up the front of his jeans. "I don't pay to fuck women. I haven't done it before. I won't start now." He wasn't trying to insult what I did, he was just stating a fact about himself. Okay, maybe he was slightly smug. Of course he didn't pay for women. What guy who looked like him did?

"Then what—" I gestured towards the card reader. If he was going to cancel the transaction, Divina would be furious. Hell, *I'd* be furious.

Unfortunately, it happened from time to time.

Fortunately, not often. Most men didn't like being banned from Flirts for life. Not to mention Divina might send someone to break their legs. This was Dusk Bay; she'd have no trouble finding someone to do just that. They might not even ask for money, but she'd pay them. Divina always paid her debts, one way or another.

He shrugged. "I paid for your company. To see you come." He leaned forward, his elbows on his thighs. "It was worth every cent." His eyes wandered up and down my naked body as though memorising every centimetre of me. "Don't tell me it's the weirdest thing that's ever happened to you."

I couldn't, because it wasn't. I appreciated every dollar, especially now. It would help me to get through the next couple of weeks of my studies. Maybe even to the end of my degree.

I shook my head. "I told you I didn't have a week." What else was he expecting from me?

"I got everything I need." He placed his hands to either side of him and pushed himself to his feet. "Take your time getting dressed. Let them think I fucked you. Let them think...whatever you want. I'll make sure that dickhead is gone before you step foot out the door."

He placed his hand on the handle, but stopped

and turned back to me. "Do me a favour. What happened here stays between us, understood?" His eyes were intense, his expression firm. He was used to telling people what to do and having them obey. He was dangerous, beyond doubt. Muscular, attractive and too sexy for his own fucking good.

And mine.

Truthfully, I would have fucked him even if he hadn't paid me. Did I regret him not touching me? Maybe a little. That in itself was a good reason to be relieved he was leaving.

I had no time to be in over my head with any guy, much less one like him.

"I'm always discreet," I said. "No one will hear about this from me."

We wouldn't have customers for long if we went around sharing what they did in private with the world. A lot of politicians and businessmen would be in big trouble if we did. Especially the married ones. Those were the ones I disliked the most. I felt sorry for their wives. If I could help it, I avoided spending time with them. That was a complication I didn't need in my life.

Storm nodded and opened the door before stepping out and closing the door with a click.

I waited for a while before pulling my clothes back on and checking my phone.

I frowned at the email sitting at the top of my inbox. It wasn't there when I started my shift, or things might have gone differently.

"Fuck," I said under my breath. Shit was about to get really, really awkward.

Chapter Three

Storm

I HIT THE GROUND WITH A THUD. THE SMELL OF soil and grass, sweat and blood made my nostrils flare. Blood surged through my adrenaline stream. Pounded.

I shoved Jay off me and jumped back to my feet.

I stalked the couple of metres to snatch up the ball, tucked it back under my arm and turned to the scrum-half. "Gonna have to do better than that."

His heart wasn't in the game. It hadn't been since he transferred from the Sydney Devils. Jayden Lang was a fucking good player. When he wanted to be.

The problem was, that wasn't often enough. The Smashers deserved a hundred percent, not a half-assed tackle delivered by an under twelve.

"Take a break," Coach shouted.

"We just started," I said under my breath, eyes still on Jay and his petulant disinterest.

He responded with a grunt and a glare before stomping off to snatch up his water bottle. He squirted water into his mouth and grimaced as though it tasted bad.

"Give him some time." Daniel Frost gave me a slap on the shoulder before he too headed over to grab up his water bottle. The big prop made no attempt to keep his voice down. That earned him a glare from Jay. Lucky him.

"It's been three months," I pointed out.

The first preseason game started on Friday night. The time for pussyfooting around was done. Correction, we'd had no time for that in the first place.

Not to mention, I was only interested in one kind of pussy, and that didn't involve feet.

Usually.

I swallowed down a mouthful of water and allowed my brain to go back to the other night. Panther. I'd bet everything my little kitten had claws. The expression on her face when she came was seared into my brain like it was branded there. The breathy little moans as she slid her fingers in and out of herself.

Thinking about her made me rock hard.

"Some take longer to acclimatise than others," Frost pointed out.

"You're the weatherman now?" I teased gruffly. "You going to tell me how long it takes before he thaws?"

Him and fucking Atlas Underwood. They were both new to the team. Both former Sydney Devils. They'd finished the last season on the top of the table. Premiership wins under their belts. And now they were playing for the Dusk Bay Smashers. We weren't the bottom dwellers. We hadn't had a wooden spoon in a decade, but we weren't on top either. Both players seemed to take that as a personal insult. Why were they here? The Devils tapped out their salary cap on all the other players. The Smashers were the best deal they could get.

In my humble opinion, they were lucky to be here. If they didn't like it, they were welcome to fuck off. They were already absent mentally. Physically wouldn't make much difference right now.

Frost shrugged. "In his own time. What does it matter, as long as he's performing on the field."

I cut him a look. That was the problem. If Jay performed on the paddock the way he was at training, we'd be fucked from the first whistle. We were better than that. He was better than that.

"Maybe you should mind your own fucking business, Stormy," Atlas sneered. "Seems like you have some work to do on your own game, if you ask me."

"No one asked you," I told him. "I don't know what they taught you over there at the Devils, but when we play rugby, a knock on isn't allowed."

I'd watched him since training started and he was sloppy with his ball placement. He could do better than he was. As a player, he was high-profile enough that if the club cancelled his contract, it would make headline news. That would be a last resort, and not a good one.

"Who died and made you a smug prick?" Atlas asked.

I grinned. "No one needed to die. I was born this awesome. Shame guys like you have to work so hard for mediocrity." I ducked as he swung. His fist narrowly missed making contact with the side of my face.

I dropped my shoulder and rammed it right into his stomach.

He staggered several steps before falling back onto the grass. I fell with him, landing on his legs before rolling away.

He was right there with me, one arm over my chest, the other landing a punch to my jaw.

Pain blossomed on the side of my face, but I punched back with my left fist, connecting with his face, his neck, anywhere I could reach.

"Fuck, break it up!" Coach Max Stanley shouted.

In the next moment, hands grabbed Atlas and me, and pulling us apart.

I got to my feet and jerked myself out of Frost and Ferris Ramsey's grips, shaking off any further attempt to touch me.

I pulled up the front of my shirt to dab at the blood under my nose. Nothing I couldn't handle. I got worse during a game.

"Save it for the field," Coach snapped. "You're supposed to smash the other guys, not each other. If you want to be a fucking team, this bullshit has to stop." He glared at me, then at Atlas.

"Sorry, Coach," I mumbled.

I wasn't sorry. Atlas took the first swing, and got what he deserved. I should have broken his nose. Or better yet, his jaw. With the right injury, he'd be out for the rest of the season.

On the other hand, the penalty for that— I'd be out too. Hell if I was going to give up my place for a dickhead like him. Whatever his problem was, I needed to stop making it mine.

Atlas muttered something and stomped away.

"That was interesting," Frost remarked. "I know you were just about to hand him his ass." He actually sounded disappointed the head coach had stepped in to stop the scuffle.

"On a silver platter," I said with a nod.

Ramsey, the Smashers' hooker, gave me a long look, his blue eyes conveying his annoyance. Whether it was with me, or with Atlas, was anyone's guess. The stocky Englishman was hard to get a read on. If he spoke, it was usually only a word or two. Most of his thoughts, he managed to convey in looks and grunts.

"Ramsey approves, don't you, Ram?" Frost teased. "He'd like nothing better than to see you smash Atlas."

Ramsey turned his disapproving look on Frost before turning and walking away.

"Atlas is right," Jay said darkly. "You're a prick. You think you own the whole fucking team. He should have broken your face. You wouldn't be so fucking smug then." He cut me a look of pure loathing.

I was only too happy to return the look. "I'd still be this smug," I said. "No way he'd be able to break my face anyway. He punches like a wet noodle."

I had two older sisters, I knew better than to claim he punched like a girl. Especially since they both played rugby and the older one, Rainy, was the first person who ever broke my nose. No one fucked with either of them and got away with it. Not even me.

Frost dropped his head back and laughed. "Wet noodle. That's hilarious."

"You know what your problem is?" Jay directed the question to Frost. "You think everything's funny, especially your boyfriend here." He gestured towards me.

That just made Frost laugh harder. "It's hysterical you think that's some kind of insult."

"I think it's kind of sad," I said. "It's obvious Jay is hiding some personal preferences, probably from himself."

Even now, sexuality was something a lot of guys on the team struggled with. As far as I was concerned, love was love. Preferences shouldn't be used as a weapon against someone else. As for denial, that just made everyone miserable.

Jay glared at me. "You think everyone wants to fuck you. You're delusional." Before I could respond, he turned and stalked away.

I shrugged. "I don't think everyone wants to fuck me, just the discerning ones."

Which brought my mind back to Panther. What was her real name? Who was she when she wasn't taking her clothes off for strangers? She was absolutely fucking gorgeous, and I got the impression she was smart. The fact she wasn't lacking in confidence added to her appeal.

In my experience, the best strippers were ones who knew exactly what they had, and were happy to share it. That was her to a T. She wasn't doing it because she had no choice. She enjoyed what she did and she was paid well to do it.

In spite of throwing myself into training, she occupied a corner of my mind, a lingering fascination coupled with the memory of her incredible body.

"There's that look again," Frost said. He snapped his fingers in front of my face. I swatted him away, but he just grinned.

"What look?" I dabbed at my face again. Atlas had opened a scab from a past training session and the blood was still trickling.

"That distracted look," Frost said. "Did you meet someone? Does she have a sister? Or a best friend?"

He looked like he was going to add something

else, but he didn't. I suspected he was going to ask if she had a brother, but Jay wasn't the only one struggling with his sexuality. If he needed my support, he only had to ask. He was one of the better guys on the team. More easy-going than the others, even if he was almost as inclined to take a swing at someone as Atlas.

"No idea," I admitted. "I met her at Flirts the other night, right after you left."

Frost frowned. "You met a girl at Flirts? Was it the chick that works behind the bar? The one with boobs for days?" He held out his hands in front of his chest, at least twice the size of the woman's actual breasts.

His eyes widened slightly and he groaned. "Wait. Was she a stripper? Did she put out? Fuck, I knew I shouldn't have left when I did. I might have gotten some action too."

A flare of annoyance in my chest had to be pushed down before I could respond. The idea of him touching my Panther made me want to take a swing at him. I had to try even harder to ignore the way my dick twitched at the thought of him fucking her while I watched.

"You left at the right time." My voice was tight.

"I didn't fuck her, we just...talked." That was all he needed to know.

"Keller," Coach called out to me. "Go and have that seen to." He waved toward my face. "Don't want you bleeding all over the paddock." As if the grass hadn't soaked up its share of blood. It had certainly seen a good amount of mine, every drop given willingly to the game I loved.

Since doing what he asked would take me away from Frost and this conversation, I nodded and replied, "Yes, Coach."

I made to step away, but stopped when he spoke again.

"I meant what I said. Keep the bullshit for the opposition. The last thing we need is to fight amongst ourselves."

I cut him a look. "Agreed, Coach." No doubt he'd tear strips off Atlas when they were alone together. Between him and Jay, they were an explosion waiting to happen. One I didn't want to be in the middle of when it went off. But I would be, because I usually was.

The Smashers were my team, my family. I wasn't going to let a couple of bad eggs ruin that for us or for our fans. They'd stuck with us through the years, while we battled to get ourselves closer to the top. For them, we would. They deserved nothing less.

I nodded to the coach and trotted across the field, the grass springing under my boots. I slipped into the locker room before heading for the infirmary.

"Coach said I needed to..."

I stopped in the doorway and stared.

What the absolute, ever loving fuck?

Chapter Four

Chelsea

I turned at the sound of his voice.

I was expecting this, but not so soon. Instead of dark jeans and t-shirt, Storm was dressed in shorts and a Smashers T-shirt. His skin glistened with sweat and blood. If he looked delicious the other night at Flirts, he looked positively tasty now.

"Hi." I greeted him with a smile before clicking over to him in my more sensible kitten heels. "Let me take a look at that."

He jerked away from me before I could touch his face. "What the fuck are you doing here?" He had the sense to keep his voice down somewhat. Whether that was for his benefit or mine, I wasn't sure.

"Professional placement," I said easily. "As part

of my sports medicine degree. Don't worry, I'm a fully qualified doctor. Medical."

"Doctor..." He echoed, eyes glazed as his brain struggled to catch up.

"Doctor Chelsea Miller." I held out my hand to him.

He stared at it. "Chelsea Miller?"

"Doctor," I reminded him, as if he would have forgotten the last thirty seconds. "Let me guess, your coach said he wanted your cheek looked at. You might need a stitch or two. Give me a moment to pull on some gloves."

"But you were... The other night..." He frowned deeply.

"Yes, I was." I snapped on my gloves and grabbed a clean washer to wipe the blood from his face. "Hold still."

He jerked away from me again and hissed, "What the fuck is going on? Is this some kind of joke? Is there a camera watching us?" He glanced around, grey eyes darker, like thunderclouds.

"Yes, it's a prank," I said sarcastically. "Women aren't really doctors. Ha ha, got you going there, didn't I?"

I could only wish this was the first time I'd had this conversation with a man.

He stared at me.

I sighed. "I really am a doctor. Would you like to see my qualifications?"

"Where's Doctor Stuart?" Storm looked around the infirmary.

"He's finishing up paperwork," I said. "You'd be surprised how much it takes to do a placement like this. Paperwork is always the worst part of the job. Is this where you tell me you'll wait and risk bleeding to death before you let me treat you?"

Also not the first time I'd had to ask something like that.

"Let's make this easy. You sit down on the treatment table and I treat you. It's really that simple."

I'd known being the new face on the team was going to be difficult, but I hadn't expected the resistance to come from him, and not over something like this. In spite of the blood, it was little more than a cut. A stitch or two in place for a couple of days would set it right. If he could put aside whatever was going on and let me do my job.

He narrowed his eyes at me. "Who are you? Why are you here? Don't bullshit me, *Panther*."

I resisted the incredibly strong urge to roll my eyes, and inhaled slowly instead.

"That's not the question, is it? You really want to

ask why I was at Flirts." Neither of us needed me to elaborate, and the last thing I needed was for someone else to walk in and overhear. I wasn't ashamed of what I did, but it was a complication I didn't need this early in the placement. Especially not when I was angling to be added to the team permanently after I graduated with my specialty degree.

Sports medicine, it was all I ever wanted to do. Treating athletes and working with professional teams. My whole life, I worked towards that goal. I sacrificed everything for it. I wasn't going to let anyone screw it up now. Especially not myself.

"I guess so," he said. "You didn't mention any of this. Did you know who I was?"

"Is that what this is about?" I scrunched up the washer in my hand, ignoring the way water dripped from it and onto the floor. "I said I'd be discreet."

"Nothing happened," he said, his expression tight.

"No, it didn't," I agreed. "Like I said, no one will hear about that from me. For the record, what I do there, I do because it pays the bills. It put me through medical school. Graduate school too. This placement I'm doing, to get up my hours of experience— I don't get paid for a minute of this. Not one. My night job is how I live. It puts food on my table. It helps fund my obsession with pot plants." I managed a small laugh and loosened my grip on the washcloth.

"As for your bigger concern," men and their egos, "Yes, I knew who you were. I had no idea I'd be accepted for this placement. It was my first choice, but it's also the first choice of most of my cohorts. I figured I'd get placed with the Dusk Bay Demons ice hockey team, or maybe the Opal Springs Ghouls. Or the Ghosts." I was babbling now. I pressed my lips together for a moment.

"The point is, if I knew I'd end up here, I wouldn't have spoken to you. I would have gone off with that guy who wanted the blowjob." I knew my words would provoke him, and they did. The skin that wasn't covered with blood turned slightly pink.

He shook his head. "You were looking at me while you were..." He glanced toward the doorway. "Taking your clothes off. You singled me out. What do you want?"

"You were standing right at the front and centre," I pointed out. "How could I miss you? Hell, how do I know you had no idea who *I* was? Maybe you were at Flirts the other night knowing I'd end up here. You wanted to make me uncomfortable for some reason."

I looked at him sideways. I knew very well all of

this was bullshit. He had no idea who I was. I was just a body for him to leer at. He would have done it to any of the dancers.

He scoffed. "How the fuck would I know a stripper was really a doctor? I've never met a doctor who was so willing to show me their pussy. Is that how you got this gig? Who did you fuck for it?"

I could have happily slapped him across the face, then pointed the finger at him for sexual harassment. But I'd heard all of this bullshit too many times before. How did I get top marks in class, had I given the professor a blowjob? How did I do so well in exams? Who had I spread my legs for?

Rather than getting angry, I was bored of the same crap I'd heard a million times before.

"I worked hard for it," I said simply. "I only flash my pussy at Flirts. You know exactly how well I get paid to do it. Because I'm fucking good at it, just like I'm good at being a doctor. Now, are you going to sit down and let me treat you, or are we going to have a problem?"

I let my hip jut out and looked at him ques- tioningly.

He still looked doubtful, but sat on the treatment table and let me wipe the blood from his jaw.

"Old wound?" I peered closely at it.

He shrugged. "One of many. I'm not doing my job if I'm not bruised and bleeding from somewhere. Or making someone else bruise or bleed."

"Of course not." I dabbed at the wound again as it went on bleeding. "That's half the fun of rugby. It's brutal and raw."

Rugby Australia was trying to find a way to minimise head injuries without taking away from the game, but a few knocks here and there didn't do the players too much harm.

"Is that why you wanted to work here?" He sat still without moving anything except his eyes. Those followed my every movement. "You like to watch men smash the shit out of each other?"

I smiled. "I like smashing in all definitions of the word. The harder, the better. Now, hold this in place and I'll get a needle and some thread. A stitch or two will do it. If you can avoid falling on your face for a few days."

He snorted. "I didn't fall on my fucking face."

"No, you probably fell on someone's fist." I pulled off my gloves, washed my hands and put on a fresh pair before starting to thread the needle with the kind of thread that would dissolve by itself in a few days. "Who did you piss of?"

"It's a Wednesday, the question is who didn't I piss off?" He sat still while I started on the first stitch.

"I'm shocked you're the kind of guy who annoys people," I said sarcastically.

He hadn't seemed that way the other night. Storm Keller wasn't the first guy to behave differently outside his native habitat. Men went to Flirts to relax as well as to enjoy the show.

"I live to please," he said with the same level of sarcasm.

"Funny, me too," I said lightly.

I snipped off the first stitch and started on the other.

He grabbed my wrist, stopping me mid-stitch. "Are you still going to...work there? If you work here full-time?" His voice was low, demanding an honest answer from me.

Apparently he hadn't believed me when I said I never fake.

I stayed perfectly still, not wanting to pull the thread through his skin and cause more damage. I didn't want to give him any excuse to complain about me. One word from a popular player like him and I'd be out on my ass before I could blink. I'd never work in the field again.

While I wouldn't object to going into general

practice, I would object to losing my dream and goal. Especially to a guy.

"I couldn't work there and travel with the team, could I now?" I said lightly.

Not to mention that the team would probably not look favourably upon a team doctor who was a stripper on the side. Working full time here, I wouldn't need a side hustle. Even if I had the energy for one.

I'd miss working at the club, and I'd miss my friends there, but it was a means to an end. When I didn't need the money from Flirts, I'd quit. Hang up my stilettos and G-string, unless I met someone I wanted to give a private show to. If a guy existed who could deal with my crazy work hours, and my confidence in bed. I knew what I liked, and I wasn't afraid to ask for it. That put some guys off, but I knew those guys weren't for me.

Who they were for, I didn't know, but it wasn't me.

"That's not a no." Storm's grip tightened on my wrist.

I looked him right in the eyes. "No. Are you happy now, or were you hoping I'd take my clothes off for you again?" If he thought he could intimidate me, he'd have to rethink.

Doctor Chelsea Miller wasn't intimidated so easily. My parents raised my older brother and me to stand up for ourselves and what we believed in. We'd fully embraced that upbringing. Neither Isaac nor I were shy, or timid. We both went after what we wanted and didn't let anything or anyone stand in our way.

I didn't miss the way Storm's eyes went darker at my words. His breath came faster. He was definitely thinking of me stripping for him. Remembering the way I touched myself and came in front of him. Remembering the way he came while I watched his hand stroking his thick, hard cock.

"You'll do that anyway," he whispered. "But next time, I'm not paying for it." He let go of my wrist and sat still again to let me finish the second stitch.

Chapter Five

Chelsea

"Remind me again why I wanted to work with the Smashers." I poured two glasses of wine and handed one to Sadie Cross, my longtime friend and housemate. There wasn't much she didn't know about me. I trusted her with all my deepest, darkest secrets. She trusted me with hers.

She took the glass and nodded her thanks before taking a sip. "Because you love rugby union? Something about rugby players' thighs?"

I sat down beside her and pulled my legs up onto the couch until my knees were almost touching my chest. "I'm not that shallow. I also like their chests."

She laughed. "I'm sure there's something about their personalities that draws you in, too. That whole rugged exterior, ready to throw all of themselves into the game, regardless of the cost to life, limb and brain cells."

We both sighed.

"Okay, that might be it. But Storm Keller is something else." The way he looked at me like he might eat me alive sent shivers of anticipation up and down my spine. I should be used to that look from guys by now, but he took it to another level. Possessive in a way I hadn't seen before.

"What about the rest of them?" Sadie asked.

"I haven't met any others yet." I sipped my wine, letting the fruity flavours sit in my mouth before I swallowed. "After Doctor Stuart was finished with the paperwork, he gave me a look around. Smashers Stadium is something else too."

"What is Doctor Stuart like?" Sadie gave me a sly look.

I snorted. "About seventy years old. Old enough not to take shit from players or people like me. But he's highly experienced. I'm going to learn so much from him."

"And from Storm Keller?" She adjusted her position on the couch, crossing her legs and leaning back against the cushions.

"I'm pretty sure he could learn a thing or two from me," I said.

Sadie smiled. "You heard it here first, folks. Chelsea Miller is going to educate the Dusk Bay Smashers fullback in the art of luuurve."

I reached over to swat her on the arm. "Who said anything about love? You of all people should know I don't have time for things like that, even if I was interested in him or anyone else." Tonight was a rare night off from study or working at Flirts.

She rolled her eyes playfully. "Fine. In the art of fucking then. You're not involved with anyone. As long as he's not involved with anyone, then I say go for it."

"What makes you think I'm interested in him? Or anyone else for that matter?" I asked.

"Because you have that expression on your face." She squinted at me. "The one that says your panties are about to melt right off. If he was here right now, you'd be jumping his bones."

"I would not," I protested. I sucked in a breath and shook my head. "He has a big enough ego without me throwing myself at him."

What about the rest of it? I couldn't deny the physical attraction between me and him was off the charts.

She hummed her disbelief. "What are you going to do then?"

"I'm going to go to work tomorrow and be a professional," I said. "I'm going to work my ass off to make sure I get a permanent spot as a team doctor. I'm not going to do anything to jeopardise that. And I'm not going to let him, or anyone else, ruin this opportunity for me. I've worked too hard for too long to let it slip through my fingers now."

"The team would be crazy not to hire you permanently," Sadie said firmly. "Although, I'm surprised the Demons weren't knocking down your door to give you a placement."

"Who says they weren't?" I asked, giving her a cagey look.

"They'd be out of their minds if they didn't," she said. "But I'm glad you got the one you wanted. I've seen how hard you work. No one deserves it more."

I reached over again, but this time to pat her hand. "That's sweet of you to say. You deserve all the good things too."

She shrugged. "Maybe. I'm happy just tending bar at Flirts and fucking around with whoever I feel like. Give me a low pressure lifestyle any day."

Sometimes I envied her. The ability to enjoy each day as it came. I could do that if I wanted to. Give up medicine and stick to getting naked for money.

On the other hand, dancing in heels was hard on a person's body after a while. I only had so many more years of wearing stilettos left in me. Medicine wasn't easy, but it was easier, if only when it came to footwear. And it involved a lot less giving of blowjobs to strangers.

"Your family must be very proud of you," she said. "Another doctor in the family. My mother would say your parents must have done something right with you and your brother."

"Yeah," I said noncommittally.

My brother was more interested in treating people after they were dead. I tried not to think too much about the ones he helped to get that way. I knew very well what he and his partners got up to. I preferred to stay out of that lifestyle. I wanted to help people, not tear literal strips off them. That was one part of my life I didn't go into detail with Sadie about. She had an inkling, but that was all. The less she knew, the better.

"Don't tell me, they wish you'd gone into bartending instead?" Sadie teased.

"My parents would be happy with whatever I did," I said. "As long as I'm enjoying my life, that's enough for them."

"They don't know you work at Flirts," she stated.

I grimaced. "Not a clue. That's not something you bring up over a family dinner. What would I say anyway? Hey, Mum, Dad, I take my clothes off and fuck men for money. Can you pass the mashed potatoes?"

Sadie giggled. "I suppose that would be awkward. I mean, mashed potatoes of all things."

I laughed. "Yes, that's the takeaway here. Deconstructed potatoes. Nothing to do with the rest of it."

"Have I ever told you what happened to Yolanda?" Sadie asked. "She worked at Flirts before you did. One night, she was in the middle of a show when an older guy walked through the door. For at least two or three minutes, he stood there staring at her, saying nothing. We've all seen that before, right?"

I nodded and gestured for her to continue.

"When he finally snapped out of it, he pointed at her and said, 'That's my daughter up there on the stage.' As you can imagine, she was absolutely mortified. He clapped a hand over his eyes, turned and tried to walk out the door. He might have bounced off the wall on the way out." She grinned.

I choked back a laugh. "That would be my worst nightmare. My father seeing me half-naked on stage.

Or coming out of one of the private rooms with a customer."

"It could be worse," she said. "He could *be* the customer."

"Sadie!" I shook my head at her. "That would definitely be worse." What people did behind closed doors was their business, but I had no interest in being intimate with my father. "What happened to Yolanda?"

"She never came back after that," Sadie said. "I don't think she could bring herself to perform. Although, safe to say, there was no way he was walking back through the door."

"Poor thing." I took another sip of wine. "I can't say I blame her. I'd probably die of embarrassment, if that's even possible."

"In this case, it probably was," she agreed. "Much better to be seen naked by guys like Storm Keller. Which brings us back to him. Does he smell as good as he looks?"

"Better," I said with a sigh. "There's nothing quite like the smell of honest sweat. It was good on him."

Not like he wasn't washed, but like he trained hard and played hard. Of course, now I was thinking about his cock and how hard it was the other night. I couldn't let him get under my skin, but he might get under the lace of my panties.

"I wouldn't be opposed to an introduction to him," Sadie said. "Or any of the guys on the team. For research, of course."

"What are you researching?" I asked.

"An in-depth comparison of the skills of rugby union players versus ice hockey players," she said. "Doesn't the world need to know which one of them fuck better? I'm happy to do the research and reveal my findings for the good of humanity."

"You're so noble," I teased. "What a sacrifice to make."

And yet, the idea of Storm touching her made me see red around the edges. I owed him nothing, and he owed me the same, but I couldn't suppress the burst of anger without a gulp of wine.

"Right?" Sadie cocked her head at me. "Are you sure you're not into him? You look kinda pissed off right now. I can stay away from him. No problem. You know the last thing I want to do is step on your toes."

My anger dissipated as quickly as it came. "I know. There's nothing to step on, really. We've had two conversations and watched each other have orgasms. That's all there is to it. Aside from that, he's a patient, and my position is tenuous until the placement is over. When I have a full-time position, I might have time to rethink being involved with him or someone else. I can't afford to lose this opportunity."

"I can't afford to lose your friendship," she said softly. "Especially over a guy. Knowing men like him, he's a total fuck boy." She rolled her hips a couple of times, miming thrusting. She could have been a dancer with those moves, but she preferred to stay behind the bar and flirt with customers from there. And disappear into private rooms with them after a shift, from time to time. Mostly, she stuck to serving drinks and keeping an eye on the dancers to make sure no one was being bothered or harassed.

"Fuck boy, ruck boy," I said with a nod.

He had exactly that vibe. Like he said, he'd never had to pay for sex. No doubt he had women throwing themselves at him right and left. Being famous and hot would do that for a guy. He didn't need me, Chelsea Miller, and he didn't need Panther. That night was nothing more than a distraction.

What about him being possessive then? Maybe we just got caught up in the moment. Us being so close to each other. Me standing up and telling him what I thought. He might not be used to that. Some guys like to be told to back the fuck off. It had the opposite effect on them. The more they were told to go away, the more they wanted to stay.

Sadie giggled. "Ruck boy, I like it. That suits him down to the ground. And you want to spend the rest of your career taking care of guys like him." She raised her glass and toasted me, her green eyes wide with humour and teasing.

When she put it that way...

I wrinkled my nose. "Does that make me some kind of crazy? That's exactly what I want to do."

"I don't think that makes you any kind of crazy," she said. "There's nothing wrong with knowing what you want and going for it. Ruck boys need love too. And medical care. You'll have your work cut out for you, that's for sure."

That was one hundred percent, without doubt, true. Storm and the rest of the team were going to keep me on my toes and I couldn't wait.

What were the rest of them like? I looked forward to finding out exactly how full my hands would be.

Chapter Six

Storm

"We could be accused of bringing the team into disrepute," Frost said as he followed me through the door into Flirts.

"That's not stopping you," I pointed out.

If he was going to be a downer, he could stay outside. He wouldn't, we both knew it. He enjoyed coming here as much as I did, possibly more. A lot could be said about Dusk Bay, but people here were discreet. Sometimes, their lives depended on it. Other times, only their livelihoods. Or their kneecaps. Either way, I was comfortable enough to swagger inside.

"Wouldn't want you to be here by yourself." He clapped me on the shoulder and stepped over to wink at the cute server behind the bar. He ordered us a couple of beers, and handed one to me.

I took a couple of gulps and turned my eyes towards the stage. The woman dancing was cute enough, but she wasn't Chelsea. Her breasts were bigger and her hair was blonde. Her enticing smile had the men around her practically panting.

"This is what I like about the place," Frost remarked. His eyes drank her in like she was tastier than the beer in his hand. "She'd look good bouncing on my cock."

Like me, he wasn't short on women willing to let him wet his dick inside them. We were usually fighting them off. But the cock wants what the cock wants.

I shrugged. "You might get your chance." She noticed him and smiled in his direction while shimmying out of her panties. Of course she had; most of Dusk Bay knew who we were. Most of them wanted a piece of us, one way or another. Some were after our money. Others, they just wanted to boast that they fucked us.

Blondie stepped to the edge of the stage and beckoned Frost over. He elbowed through the crowds toward her, ignoring the angry glares on the way past. Smiling, she gripped the front of his shirt to pull him closer, before draping one of her legs over his shoulder, her pussy right in his face.

He knew better than to touch, but that didn't stop him from smiling and visibly inhaling her scent.

"He's such a slut." I hadn't seen Dallas Gregory, the team's second-rower, until he stepped out of the crowd towards me.

"Pot, meet kettle," I said pointedly. Dallas got around as much as the rest of us did. Personally, I didn't know what women saw in him. He was a grumpy prick at the best of times. Always with a massive chip on his shoulder. He was as dedicated to the team as I was. He had that much going for him.

Dallas shrugged. "I'm not the one with a face full of pussy. He doesn't seem to be hating it."

He certainly didn't. Frost was grinning, his hand now gripping the dancer's thigh. If he wanted to, he could flick out his tongue and lick her pussy. If the bouncers weren't standing so close, watching carefully, he probably would.

The dancer lowered her leg from him and whispered something in his ear. He nodded vigorously before she took his hand and led him in the direction of one of the private rooms.

"Someone is getting laid tonight," Dallas remarked. He seemed to have his eye on a dark-haired woman behind the bar. She was pouring drinks and chatting to the customers.

"Go for it," I said. "Might help you to lighten up." I won't lie, I could do with getting laid myself. But not to some random woman.

The more I tried to push her out of my mind, the more I thought about Chelsea. I knew there was more to her on the night we met, but I hadn't expected her to be an actual fucking *doctor*. She couldn't have shocked me more. Not if she said she had three breasts and two pussies. Although, two pussies would have been interesting. It might have been fun to share her with someone like Frost. Hell, it still might. She had three holes and two hands. Plenty to go around.

If I was willing to share her with anyone else.

The thought of her body made my balls heavy. My cock wanted to be inside her more than any woman I ever met. In theory, that made her danger-ous. Someone I should stay away from. I had enough on my plate without being distracted.

Tell that to my cock though. If she was right in front of me, I'd bend her over a table and slam into her.

"We could all do with a good fuck," Dallas said, distracted with the view. That was until Chelsea stepped out on the stage. His face swivelled, wide eyes now locked on her. His jaw dropped like someone recently oiled the hinges.

I resisted the urge to punch him in the face. It wasn't his fault he reacted to her that way. Most of the guys in the club stopped to stare at her. Hell, my cock was instantly hard, and she was fully dressed.

Should I be here watching the woman who might potentially be our future team doctor get naked? Maybe, maybe not. Was I going to leave? Hell no. She was exactly why I came here tonight. To see her. To watch her dance for me. So she could understand I intended to make her mine.

Beer all but forgotten in my hand, I shouldered my way through the crowds, to the edge of the stage. As close to her as I could get without the bouncers tossing me out on my ass.

Close enough to watch her. Close enough to put myself between her and anyone else. She could take her clothes off for all of these men, show them her pussy, but when she was done, she was mine.

I found Dallas beside me, his eyes dark. If he stared at her any more, he was going to need to wipe the drool off his chin. The tent in the front of his pants was as obvious as mine. I ignored the way seeing him like that made me harder.

I tried to ignore the mental image of him slamming into Chelsea while she was on all fours on the stage. Her back arched, crying out in pleasure as he thrust his cock deep inside her.

If I kept thinking like this, I was going to lose my load in my jeans. I'd never lost control like that, and I wasn't going to start now. If I did, I'd add punishing her to the list of things I was going to do to her. Her ass would look even more perfect with my red handprint in the centre of each cheek. Her throat would be exquisite with bruises from my palm and fingers.

Did she like it rough? If she didn't yet, she'd soon learn. I'd teach her to like the things I liked. She'd take everything I gave her and scream for more.

Chelsea noticed us both standing there and the sides of her mouth tightened slightly. The expression only lasted a moment before her smile was back. She was nothing if not professional. In spite of our last conversation, she was going to put on a show for me. Entice me. Even with all the other guys present, she was taking her clothes off for me. When she showed her pussy, it would be for my eyes.

My tongue slid deliberately over my lips, silently telling her how tasty she looked. I wanted to slide into her then and there, but I'd have to wait. Let her tease me first. Let her make me harder. Then I'd take her. Claim her. Own her.

She mimicked my expression, licking her lips before gripping the pole and spinning around it. The muscles in her arms strained with the effort. She made it look ridiculously easy. Like anyone highly skilled did.

We had a similar pole in our training gym. When it first appeared, the guys all thought it was there for a laugh. They stopped laughing when, one by one, they tried to use it, to hold themselves there with upper body strength. They quickly realised it was a lot more difficult, a lot more athletic than they thought.

Okay, I admit to thinking the same until I gave it a go. I was nowhere near as graceful as Chelsea, but I appreciated the strength she had to do what she did. And she did it in stiletto heels, while sliding her clothes off, garment by garment.

First, a pale pink crop top with a picture of a strawberry between her breasts, then her skimpy shorts. Her hair was held back in a pair of pigtails that made her look younger than she was. Sweeter.

There was nothing sweet about her in a black lace bra and G-string. She was pure sex on heels. A walking orgasm. Her body was perfection. I wanted to trickle chocolate onto her and lick it all off. I wanted her on her knees, her mouth around me while I came down her throat. I wanted to slide my cock into the gap between her breasts and come on her face.

"Jesus fucking Christ," Dallas whispered. Evidently, I wasn't the only one having those thoughts.

I grunted my agreement. The blood seemed to have abandoned my head and I was now only thinking with my cock and balls. Both of them wanted to touch her badly. They ached to feel her hands, her mouth, her pussy, her ass.

She watched us both as she danced, teasing that she was going to take off her bra before she finally did. She twirled it over her shoulder, tossed it and turned around, displaying her perfect breasts and rosy pink nipples. Both taut and erect for me. Ready to be sucked and nipped.

I slid a look over to Dallas. He stood with his mouth slightly open, eyes wide. His hand hovered near the bulge in his pants. He looked ready to pull out his cock and get himself off here and now. A couple of guys were already doing exactly that, eyes on her, their hands wrapped around their lengths.

I had more restraint than that. Barely.

For the most part, I ignored the other men around me, even when they pulled out their money and threw the notes onto the stage at her feet. I meant what I said when I told her I wouldn't pay to fuck her. I had something else in mind. A warmup. I'd show her my appreciation, but not like this. I'd be more subtle about it.

Chelsea turned her back on us and slid her panties off before kicking them aside. She aimed for the back of the stage, but they stopped in front of me. I stopped to snatch them up and shove them in my pocket before grinning at her. I gave her a look that said 'if you want them back, you're going to have to come and get them.'

She shook her head slightly and smiled, before spinning around the pole again, her legs apart to display her pussy to the adoring crowd.

I didn't miss the way she glistened. She was as turned on as I was. Getting ready for me to take her. And I would. In time.

She wriggled and danced for a while longer, her breasts bouncing, before scooping up her bra and clothes. She hesitated long enough to give me a good look at a rear hole, then straightened up and hurried backstage.

"She won't be long," I said to Dallas.

He frowned at me. "What makes you think—"

"I don't think, I know," I said. I started to step away, but stopped and looked back at him. "You want to fuck her, don't you? Come on then."

He gave me a funny look, but followed me through the crowds and back to the quieter side of the club.

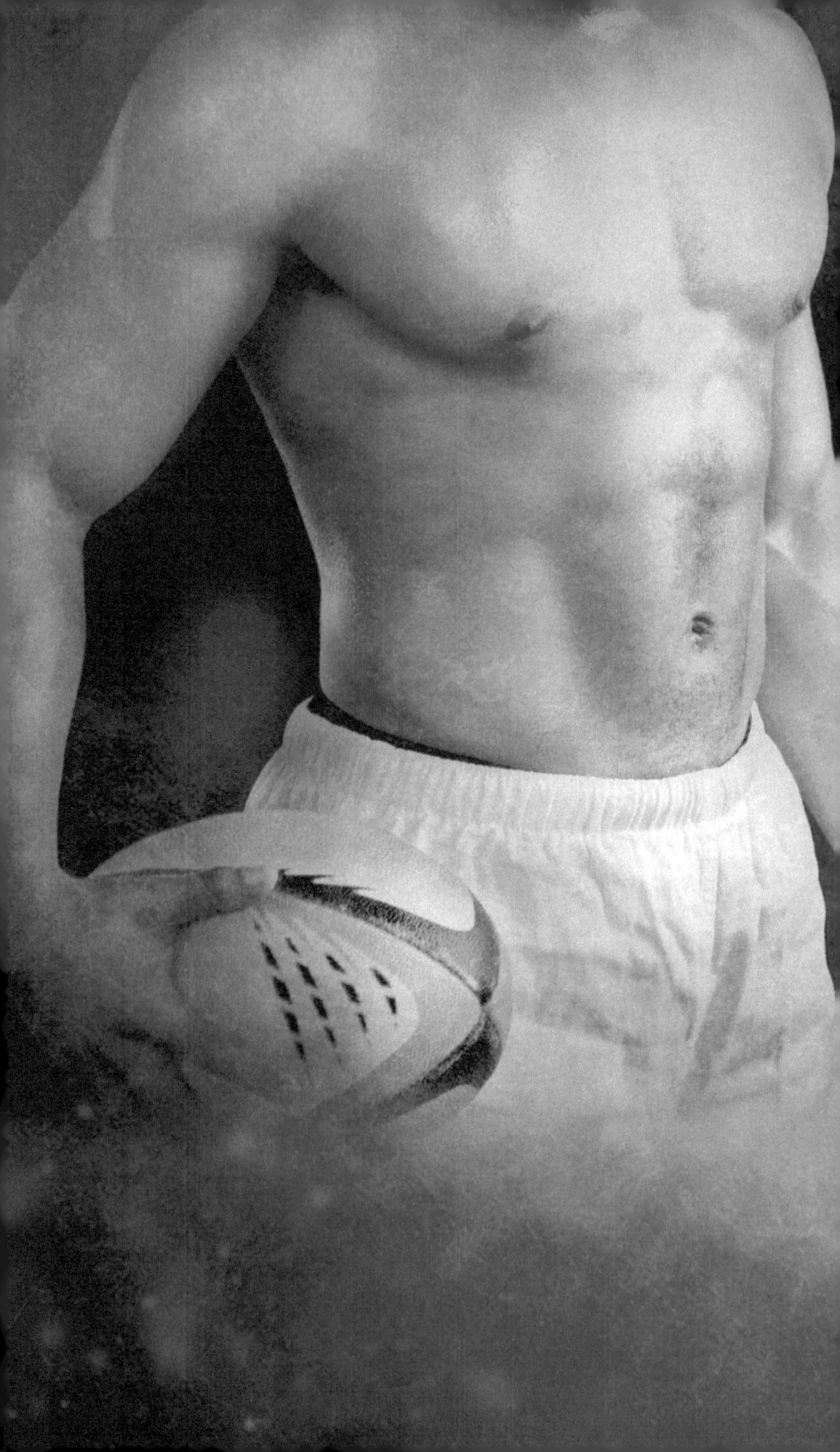

Chapter Seven

Chelsea

I wasn't surprised to see Storm waiting for me, or that Dallas Gregory was with him. Neither of them took their eyes off me during my whole performance.

Just by looking, I couldn't tell if Dallas knew who I was outside of Flirts. If I had to guess, I'd say he didn't.

The way Storm's predatory gaze clung to me like a steel trap was subtly different to the last time he was here. Knowing, but wary. Waiting for the play he was sure would come. Or the moment to pull off a play of his own.

Dallas looked at me like I was little more than a beautiful body. A woman to lust after, to covet, but not one he recognised. Should I enlighten him?

Possibly, but if Storm hadn't, it was better to keep my mouth shut for now. He'd find out sooner or later. In the meantime, I was going to roll with whatever Storm had in mind.

"Hi," I greeted cheerfully. "You boys like the show?"

Storm's jaw worked from side to side a couple of times, as if he expected me to greet him some other way. If that was the case, that was his problem.

"Yeah," Dallas said simply. Judging by the bulge in his pants, he was having difficulty thinking with the head on his shoulders. That was on par for the course around here. Men left their vocabularies at the door.

I placed a hand on his bicep and smiled right at him. Up close, he smelled like leather and soap. His arm was hard under my palm, muscles straining against his sleeves. His hazel eyes were so dark, they were almost green, except for flecks of gold here and there.

"That's great. You boys getting a drink?"

Storm gave me a look as if to ask what I was up to.

I turned my best innocent smile on him. I wasn't up to anything. I was doing my job. Charming the customers. Getting them to loosen up.

"I've got something else in mind." He jerked his head towards the private rooms.

Just as he did that, Daniel Frost stepped out with Ivy, a grin plastered on his face.

"You guys are everywhere," I said so only Storm could hear.

He shrugged. "We like it here. Go on, my money is still good." Apparently he was also determined to separate my two jobs. He wasn't looking at me like a patient would look at a doctor. He was looking at me like I was a possession, to be used however he wanted to. He was making no attempt to pretend otherwise.

His attitude would have pissed off Doctor Chelsea, but the Chelsea who'd been selling herself here for the last couple of years was intrigued. Every time I thought I'd seen and done everything, I was proven wrong. Was that the case here?

I stepped towards the door to a clean private room, and gave both guys a smile over my shoulder. I opened the door and stepped inside, leaving them to follow.

Before the door closed behind them, I caught a glimpse of an older man, his gaze intent on me. Dark eyes watched silently, drinking me in before he disappeared from sight. I'd seen him in Flirts a few times before, but he always kept his distance. For no reason I could identify, he always put me on edge. I couldn't turn away fast enough, my smile for the other two men.

Dallas looked slightly dazed, but Storm was completely in control of himself. Certain he was in control of the situation.

I didn't bother to correct him. Let him think he was the boss for now. We both knew if he crossed the line, I'd stop playing. Hands on my ample hips, I stood with hooded eyes while he closed the door, and waited for him to tell me what he expected me to do.

He glanced at me before walking over to the card reader and punching in the details. He lifted it to show me an amount larger than the other night. With that, I may never have to work at Flirts ever again. Hell, if he kept paying me like that, I could retire.

"I thought you weren't going to pay for me again," I said easily. Throwing his words back at him might not be a good idea, but I couldn't help provoking him. I wanted to see what he'd do. How he'd react. If I could make him lose control, even slightly.

Storm leaned back against the wall and crossed his arms. His expression gave away little. Certainly no anger or annoyance. "I'm not paying for me to fuck you. I'm paying to watch him fuck you." He nodded towards Dallas.

Dallas gaped. His eyes narrowed for a moment, but then widened again. His jaw snapped shut, eyes darker than before, hungrier. He was a much easier read than his teammate. He wanted me. The circumstances didn't matter. He'd claim me, with or without money involved.

"Take your clothes off," Storm said to me. "Show him what my money is getting him."

I stepped away from him, to the middle of the room and focused all of my attention on the second-rower. Like I had the other night, I did a slow striptease, removing the clean underwear I just put on. I didn't bother to ask Storm for my panties. Let him keep them. I had plenty of other pairs. I suspected he'd refuse anyway. He'd keep them like a trophy. A sign of some kind of connection between us.

"So fucking beautiful," Dallas whispered.

"Why don't you lie down on the bed?" Storm said to him. He turned to me and added, "I want to see you suck him off."

Dallas scrambled onto the bed and lay back, eyes half-closed. Cock erect as a goal post.

"Crawl to him," Storm insisted.

I knelt on the edge of the bed and started a very

slow crawl toward the other player. Glancing over at Storm, I undid the front of Dallas' pants and peeled the sides back until his erection sprang free. I palmed his hard length, caressing the vein that ran underside until he groaned and bucked his hips, thrusting between my fingers.

"Fuck," he moaned.

I palmed his balls for a moment or two before reaching over to the table beside the bed to pick up a condom.

"What are you—" Storm started.

"House rules," I said. "Outside of Flirts, we can do what we want. Here we use condoms."

He looked annoyed, but nodded for me to continue.

I tore the packet open with my teeth and rolled the condom down Dallas's cock. Lying half over him, I teased his head with my tongue before lowering my mouth and taking him all the way down my throat.

"Fucking hell," Dallas breathed. "So good." He rolled his head back and closed his eyes, his lips turned up. Slowly, with more control than I would have thought he had, he bucked his hips, fucking my mouth.

Storm groaned softly. His balls must have been aching. Cock throbbing and engorged with blood.

In the corner of my eye, I saw him kneel down on the bed before he rolled me so he could part my legs and lower his mouth to my pussy.

The first swipe of his tongue sent a shiver all the way through me. Many of my customers didn't care whether I came or not, but he clearly knew what to do with his mouth. He expertly found my clit and teased it mercilessly, while slipping a couple of thick fingers inside me.

Dallas fucked my mouth a little faster now. Control gradually slipping away even though the expression on his face spoke of how hard he was trying to cling to it.

I massaged his balls and stroked the skin around his prostate, stimulating him further while I gagged with every thrust.

He groaned. His back arched and his cock pumped harder between my lips before a squirt of warm cum filled the condom.

He flopped back against the mattress, panting lightly. He stayed like that for about ten seconds before he jerked his cock out of my mouth.

"Fuck." He slid the condom off and tossed it aside. It hit the wall with a wet splat before sliding down and landing on the floor. "Fuck." He rolled away from me and looked at me like he'd never seen me before.

"Fuck." He did up the front of his pants and got to his feet.

"Dallas, what the hell, dude?" Storm lifted his mouth from my pussy when I was way too close to coming.

Dallas shook his head in disgust. Whether it was with me, Storm, himself or all of the above, I couldn't tell.

"I don't fuck whores," he said finally. "I *don't pay to fuck.*"

"You didn't pay, I did," Storm pointed out. His breath tickled my clit.

"Same fucking thing." Dallas wrenched the door open and hurried out of the room, letting it swing closed behind him.

I sighed to myself. The same thing happened to me several times before. Guys got caught up in the moment and regretted it immediately afterward. In this case, though, things could get very complicated. Sooner or later, he'd see me at the stadium and remember this.

"He doesn't know, does he?" I asked.

"He will," Storm said, as though it was no big

deal at all. He lowered his mouth and went back to swiping his tongue over my clit. "Come for me."

Things might get ugly later, but for now I might as well let myself go and come on his mouth, on his dollar. I closed my eyes, spread my knees wider and enjoyed the way he was feasting on me. He groaned from deep in the back of his throat, suggesting I was the most delicious thing he'd ever tasted.

As if Dallas leaving never happened, I was quickly back on the edge of coming. I was right there before Storm pulled his mouth away. He grinned at me, letting me come down before diving back in and driving me closer again.

The man knew exactly how to play a woman. How to drive me absolutely wild.

Before he could pull back again, I came hard and fast against his mouth, the whole room disappearing as I was caught up in a wave of pure bliss. I cried out loudly. Loud enough for my throat to hurt. Loud enough that if the room wasn't soundproofed, the whole club would have heard. Loud enough to satisfy an ego as big as his.

He went on licking and sucking my clit until I came all the way back down to earth.

Swiping the back of his hand over his mouth, he

undid his jeans and pulled out his cock. He knelt beside me and worked himself quickly.

"I'm going to put this inside you," he said, his voice strained. "But not here. Not like this." He pumped harder, hips moving hypnotically back and forth.

He let out a low moan and came, squirting cum across my stomach and one of my breasts. Like warm cream, it lay across me, making my skin sticky.

He slumped forward, pumped his cock a couple more times and let it go. "I'm going to come inside you. You're going to take every drop and you're going to thank me for it."

He lifted his head, his jaw firm. "You belong to me, Chelsea Miller. I'm going to own you. Every centimetre of your body is mine. Every last bit. When the time is right, I'm going to claim you and you're going to scream my name."

I raised my eyebrows. "Is that so?"

He did his pants back up, lowered himself down onto all fours and crawled up beside me. "It's very much so. You're mine and I'm going to prove that to you."

He was nothing if not absolutely confident in every word that came out of his mouth. If I wasn't careful, he might convince me. As it was, I didn't let down my guard.

"What about Dallas?" I asked.

Storm's gaze shifted towards the door, then back again. "He'll come around when he has time to calm down. He's...volatile."

"I noticed that," I said dryly. "You paid for him to fuck my mouth. Do you usually do that with women you think you own?"

He moved before I could blink, wrapping his hand around my throat.

"I don't *think* I own you. I *know* I own you. I let him fuck you because I wanted him to. I wanted to watch you. I want to watch him do it again. Some of the others..." He trailed off. Whatever he was thinking, he seemed to like the idea.

"I'm not your fuck toy," I told him.

His hand around my throat shouldn't have felt arousing, but it did. At the same time, I was ready to knee him in the groin. If he thought I was some kind of shrinking violet who couldn't look after herself, he needed to think again. I could hurt him in ways he couldn't even imagine. All without breaking a sweat.

He laughed, short and dark. "Sweetheart, that's exactly what you are. My fuck toy. Maybe I should pay to fuck you." He leaned in and whispered,

"Maybe I should buy you." He pinched my nipple with his spare hand.

I whispered back, "You couldn't afford me."

He rolled us over until he was lying with his body on top of mine and smiled. "Then I'll take you."

Before I could respond, he rolled off the bed and stood. "I'll see you at work tomorrow." He took a long, lingering look at my body before opening the door and stepping out of the room.

Chapter Eight

Chelsea

Doctor Stuart glanced appraisingly at me as I stepped through the door. One greyed eyebrow was cocked with a hint of concern.

"Late night cramming for exams," I explained. No amount of makeup could cover the weary look in my eyes, worse luck.

He nodded, apparently taking my words as the truth. Being exhausted was a common state of being for students doing practical training. Essays and exam study didn't stop because we were out working in our fields.

"Right, well, we have several physicals to work through this morning. Standard preseason checks to make sure the players are in form to play." He waved at the screen in front of him. "This process will take a few days, but we have to be absolutely certain to cover everything."

Of course we did. If we missed anything now, the players could suffer. At best, we could lose our jobs. At worst, they could worsen an existing injury, and we'd be sued for negligence. As one of my university lecturers used to say, "Meticulous, meticulous, meticulous." Us students used to mimic him, but he wasn't wrong.

"Great," I said with my perky demeanour firmly in place. "Who do we have first?"

Please say it's not Storm or Dallas.

I wasn't ready to face either of them. I didn't *think* they'd tell the team what I did at night, but shit could get awkward really fast. Having to perform a physical on a man who thought he owned me, was about as awkward as things could get. Not to mention seeing one who was ashamed of having been intimate with me.

Past Chelsea should have turned them down, but that was a problem for future Chelsea.

"Daniel Frost," Doctor Stuart said. "I believe you're familiar with the players and their positions."

Was that a deliberate choice of words, or was I

reading more into what he was saying? Probably the latter. Doctor Stuart didn't seem like the type to use innuendos, especially in this context.

"I know what they all play, and I understand the strain each position can put on specific parts of their bodies," I said, trying to sound as clinical as possible. "I read through the file you sent me, outlining their past injuries and anything that may be an ongoing concern. I recall that Frost broke his collarbone in the season before last, that could have ended his career." It hadn't, but he'd been out for a while as he recovered.

"We're fortunate some of the players follow orders when they're told to take it easy," Doctor Stuart said gruffly. "Most of them, if I'm honest. None of them want a career-ending injury. Or any injury, for that matter. They rail against restrictions, but when it comes down to it, this is their job. If they can't perform, then their rugby playing days are over. That's quite an incentive to behave."

I smiled. "I can just imagine you've had your share of...frustration."

He chuckled. "You could say that. But every single one of them knows we're here for them. We want the same thing they want. For them to be back out on the field as soon as possible. The only way for that to happen is for them to listen to us." He hesitated.

"Is this where you say they may not let me boss them around because I'm a woman?" I asked.

"They may push back harder against you than they would against me," he agreed. "Not just because you're a woman. You're also new, and still a student. Give them some time; they'll learn to respect you. I recommend not showing them any fear. The moment you do that, you've lost them. I wouldn't like to see that happen. What I've seen of your work so far, you're very promising. I think you'll fit in here. However, before I can give my recommendation, I need to be sure you can work with these men. If you let them walk all over you, they will."

"I haven't let anyone walk all over me yet," I said.

Let Storm think whatever he wanted to think, and say whatever he wanted to say. When he was here, under my care, he'd do what I told him to. No matter how much he hated the idea.

He vaguely patted my hand. "I didn't think you would. This job isn't an easy one, but it's very rewarding. We work with some of the best rugby players on the face of the planet. Elite athletes who put two hundred percent into everything they do. They need to be precise and so do we. We need to be more accurate than a Swiss clock. Three hundred percent of the time. If you're willing to put in the work, you'll reap the rewards."

"I'm ready to reap." I grinned. "And I'm ready to work my ass off." If anyone doubted I could do this, they'd be proven wrong quickly enough.

"But your ass is so cute," a voice said from the doorway.

I turned to see Daniel Frost leaning against the door frame, arms folded over his chest, legs crossed at his ankles. Boyish mischief danced in those blue eyes of his. His blond hair was cut short, making him look more like a male model than a rugby union player.

He blinked a couple of times and frowned, as though trying to figure out where he knew me from.

Doctor Stuart clicked his tongue. "What have we said about sexually harassing the medical staff?"

Frost slid him a sly look and a grin. "Only harass the cute ones?" He held up a hand. "I don't mean to imply that you're not cute, Doctor. You're adorable. In an old-enough-to-be-my-grandfather kind of way."

Doctor Stuart snorted softly. "Why don't you sit down on the treatment table? Doctor Miller can get started looking you over. I'll be back in a couple of minutes."

"Doctor Miller, hmmm?" Frost said after Doctor

Stuart had left. He lay down, his hands laced under his head, ankles crossed. A faint smile curved the corners of his mouth, like he knew something I needed to catch onto ASAP.

"That's right," I said. "You can call me Chelsea if you want to." I pulled on a pair of gloves and rolled the sphygmomanometer over to test his blood pressure.

"You can call me Frost," he said. "Unless you prefer Daddy." He grinned again, popping a dimple in each cheek.

"Do you flirt with all the doctors like this?" I gestured for him to push up his sleeve and placed the cuff around his muscular bicep.

"Only the ones I've seen naked," he said, making no attempt to keep his voice down. "Yes, I recognise you. Not gonna lie, it took me a minute. You look different with your clothes on." His eyes narrowed just a fraction.

"You look different when you're not walking out of a private room," I retorted. If he was offering a thinly veiled threat, he'd get one in return.

His face paled slightly. "So we can agree to keep things professional?"

I leaned in and whispered, "I won't tell if you don't. Now, keep still and think less stressful thoughts, or your blood pressure is going to be compromised by this...conversation."

"Whatever you say, Doctor." He was immediately still, stiff as a board. "You know it was only..."

"I know," I said. "Nothing to be ashamed of. You really need to relax. The last thing you want is for me to say you can't play because your blood pressure is too high. Let's talk about something else. Puppies."

"Puppies?" He frowned.

"Yes, puppies. Everyone loves puppies, don't they? They're so cute and furry, and they never judge your life choices. I mean, they don't care if you eat Nutella and pickles together."

He made a face and laughed. "You eat Nutella and pickles?"

I smiled. "Of course not. I'm just saying a puppy wouldn't judge you if you wanted to." I checked the blood pressure machine. "That's better." I took off the cuff and gestured for him to sit up so I could listen to his heart.

"I wouldn't judge you either," he said. "I don't mean about...what you eat. I mean, if that's what you want to do..."

"It's just a job," I said. "Something to do before I work here permanently. That's all. No big deal."

"Right, no big deal," he said softly. "Do you—"

"Do it outside of the club? Not for money." I slipped on a stethoscope and pressed the bell to his back.

I probably couldn't hear him gulp through the stethoscope, but I imagined I could.

"So you...go out on dates and shit like that?" he asked. His tone was tentative, but curious. Wanting to know but perhaps not wanting to be offensive. Or perhaps hoping I wouldn't ask too many questions in return.

I should start a blog about my life as a stripper. I could answer all of the big questions I'd been asked before, or the ones people skirted around.

On the other hand, right then, I had more than enough on my plate without taking on another project. Not even one that would reduce the stigma around one of the oldest professions in the world.

"Yes, I do, but you need to be quiet so I can listen," I said.

He complied for a minute or two, until I stepped away and put the stethoscope aside.

"Your heart sounds good and strong," I said.

"That's what my mother always says," he said, his chest puffed out proudly. "That I'm full of heart. The guys say I'm full of shit, but at least my mother loves me." He looked rueful.

I laughed softly. "Of course she does. You seem sweet." Especially in comparison to Storm and Dallas. I got the impression Frost was a fraction more innocent than they were. I suspected underneath he was as worldly as me. A guy didn't play a sport like rugby union at a professional level while being sheltered. He'd be used to giving and taking hard knocks, literally and figuratively. I had to give him credit for not letting them wear him down. I hoped they never would, that he was never jaded.

"I am sweet," he said. "You want to hang out with me some time?"

His words hung in the air for a moment before I absorbed them. Or maybe I was giving him a chance to take them back. He seemed like the kind of guy who lived in the moment, impulsively jumping into anything with both feet. While I respected that, I knew sometimes it was helpful to have a way out. Spontaneity sometimes came with instant regret.

I gave him a sideways look. "Are you asking Doctor Chelsea, or the woman from Flirts?"

He matched my look. "Are they so different? So far, I've seen a beautiful, intelligent woman who thinks I'm sweet. I'd like to get to know you better." He must have figured out what my concern was, because he added, "With your clothes on."

Should I have assumed he only wanted to get me naked and fuck me? Potentially not, but I'd seen it a metric shit ton of times before. What made him any different?

He had a similar reputation to most of the guys on the team: ruck boy, fuck boy. In it for an hour or two, not a lifetime. Us hanging out might be nothing more than a fun roll in the sheets. Okay, I admit that sounded like exactly what I needed. No pressure, no strings. Just fun.

"Sure," I said finally. "Why not? It can't hurt to get to know the players better." There were no rules against spending time with them, as long as it didn't get serious. Unless I'd turned into a bad judge of character overnight, there was more to him than a guy who tackled other men for a living.

"It definitely can't," he agreed. "I have a feeling you're going to be very popular with lots of the guys on the team." Again he added, "With your clothes on." But then straight after that, "Or off. Both are good."

"I see I'm going to have to keep my eyes on you," I teased. "Now, we should get on with the physical, or Doctor Stuart will wonder what we've been up to."

"He'll know we didn't get up to anything dirty,"

Frost stated. "If we did, I would have made you scream so loud the whole stadium heard it."

I shook my head at his cockiness and continued my careful physical examination of the muscular prop.

Chapter Nine

Chelsea

"You found it," Frost said, like he was surprised. It was a cafeteria, not a clit.

I held up my phone and waved it from side to side. "And I'm not even late."

"Punctuality is so hot." He jumped up from his chair and pulled out mine for me.

"It really is." I gave him a look before I sat and placed my lunch and coffee on the table in front of me. I didn't need him opening doors and pulling out chairs, but his doing so was sweet. "I'd never under-sell the importance of being on time."

"I'll bear that in mind." He sat back in his own chair and started to open his lunch. Salad and chicken breast. Healthy, if not exciting.

I made a show of unwrapping my ham, cheese

and mayonnaise sandwich and placing my chocolate cupcake beside it. I worked out so I could eat shit like that. Not enough to lose all of my curves, but some. Whatever. Unlike him, I had no one counting my calories for me. If they tried, I'd tell them to fuck all the way off. Life was too short not to enjoy a cupcake once in a while.

"How was the rest of your morning?" he asked before pushing some lettuce into his mouth. "I presume it went downhill after I left."

I snorted softly and bit into my sandwich. "Absolutely." I chewed carefully and swallowed. "All of those hard bodies. Such a stressful morning."

The couple of players after him were more reserved, answering questions and doing as they were told before hurrying out of the infirmary. All very businesslike. All guys I recognised from past games and media interviews, not from the club. One was married and, from what I heard, the other was happily engaged. Not the kind of guys to bother with strip clubs.

"Are you trying to make me jealous?" Frost asked.

"You want to touch those hard bodies too?" I asked, slightly teasing, but mostly curious.

His face turned slightly pink. "It's not... I don't...

I don't know," he said finally. "Kinda. But I want to touch you too. I mean, women."

I nodded. "Figuring out preferences can be confusing. Especially when you're surrounded by so much testosterone." The pressure to be one of the guys must be immense. Looking at the wrong one, the wrong way could get you punched in the head. It would be easier to go with the flow, as they say. Not as satisfying, but safer.

"Yeah." He stuffed a large piece of chicken into his mouth, punctuating his unease.

"Just so you know, I won't judge you," I said. "You don't judge me for doing what I do."

He cracked open a bottle of water and took a gulp. "Nope, why would I? Before I was contracted to play for the Smashers, I delivered pizza at night and couriered parcels during the day. You do whatever you have to, y'know?"

"I do know," I agreed.

I had a feeling I knew a lot more than he did. This was Dusk Bay, a perfectly ordinary looking city run by organised crime bosses like Reuben Brantley. Frost could have been delivering severed heads without knowing. I wouldn't have even been slightly surprised. Did he know about that side of the city? I had a feeling he didn't, and I wouldn't be the one to fill him in. Not now anyway.

"Were you one of those naked pizza delivery guys?" I teased.

He chuckled. "I don't think that's a thing, but I totally would have. Remind me to deliver pizza to your place one day." He winked and went on eating.

"It could be a thing," I said. "Whoever starts a business like that would probably rake in the cash."

"Especially if you're doing the delivering," he said. "I'd pay to see that. Or better yet—" He leaned forward and whispered, "I'd pay to eat pizza off you. You'd be delicious. I'd lick you clean."

"I'm sure you would," I said. "But body shots are better."

He grimaced. "I'm really hard right now." He shifted in his seat and adjusted himself.

I leaned over and patted his bicep. "That's what you get for talking dirty to me."

"I did bring this on myself, didn't I?" he said.

"Yes. Yes you did." I opened my cupcake and bit into the icing.

"It would be inappropriate of me to suggest I lick icing off your chin, wouldn't it?" he asked.

"Given we both work here, yes it would," I agreed.

"If we weren't here, would it be appropriate then?" He cocked his head at me.

"It would depend on where we were," I said. "It might be inappropriate at Flirts too, but if we were, say, out on a date, then it would probably be appropriate."

He absorbed my response and nodded. "Then we better do that. Go out on a date. If you want to, I mean. I like you and I think you like me. I wouldn't mind finding out where this could go."

I glanced around to make sure no one was listening before I asked, "It doesn't bother you that half of Dusk Bay has seen me naked?" Not to mention the percentage of the male population of the city who paid to fuck me. Having sex with someone like me was one thing. Being involved in a relationship, even a friendship, was another. Some guys couldn't look past their own jealousy.

"I don't care." He shook his head. "It doesn't bother me if they've *all* seen you naked. I have endorsements for underwear, and I did an ad once where they photographed my naked ass and put it in the pages of a magazine." He pulled out his phone, tapped on the screen and turned around to show me.

"Your ass is adorable," I said. And now I wanted to bite it. Or lick tequila off his ass cheeks.

"It's okay." He shrugged and put his phone back down on the table. "Not as nice as yours." He hesitated for a moment. "Are you going to keep...you know?"

"Working at Flirts? Only until I have a permanent job, hopefully here with the Smashers."

"Right," he said slowly. "Good. Like I said, I like you. I don't want to have to go there every night and punch out every guy who looks at you the wrong way."

"That's sweet," I said, "But the bouncers would throw you out at the first swing."

"Then I'd have to follow them out and beat the crap out of them outside," he said unapologetically.

"I think you like your job too much to risk it," I said.

"It's only at risk if I get caught," he pointed out. "So, dinner on Monday night?"

"I might have to check my schedule," I said.

He picked up my phone and tapped on the screen. "You should put a passcode on this. Anyone could look at your stuff." He opened the calendar and pressed on Monday. Squinting, he tapped in 'dinner with Daniel Frost' for six PM. He closed the calendar and opened the contacts app to tap in his phone number. With a sly grin, he pressed on his number to call himself.

"There, we have each other's phone number and a time."

"You're right, I should put in a passcode," I said dryly. "Fine, dinner at six. Text me where and I'll meet you there."

"I don't mind picking you up." He looked as though he was ready to argue. Like he should insist on being chivalrous, because it was the manly thing to do. Or something similar.

"And I don't mind meeting you there," I said. I'd learned long ago not to be trusting, no matter how sweet a guy seemed to be. One minute they were asking you out and giving you flowers, and the next they were turning up at your place expecting a fuck. Or taking photos of you through the curtains. Or threatening your life because of who you happened to be related to.

"I want to punch whoever made you feel like you can't trust me," he said. His expression darkened with annoyance.

"It's no big deal," I said lightly.

He leaned forward, elbows on the table. "It is a big deal. I'll do whatever I have to do to earn your trust. If I do anything to break it, I'll punch myself."

He raised his fist and mimed driving it into his own face.

"Don't make promises you might not be able to keep," I told him. "Shit happens, whether you want it to or not. Besides, you don't know if you can trust me."

"Of course I do," he said easily. "What is it they say? 'Trust me, I'm a doctor.' If I can't trust you, who can I trust?"

I supposed he had a point. Doctors were supposed to be dependable and reliable. I strove to be both of those things. On the other hand, blind faith sometimes led to disappointment. If he was going to jump into anything with me, I needed him to have his eyes wide open. He needed to understand who the real Chelsea Miller was, not just Doctor Chelsea, or Chelsea the sex worker. Rose coloured glasses weren't good for anyone.

"I'm starting to think you're too sweet for your own good," I said.

The best thing I could do for him would be to walk away. Especially given my last conversation with Storm Keller. Would he give Frost a hard time for going out with me? Probably, and that would create tension the team didn't need.

Admittedly, while I didn't want them at odds

with each other, Storm didn't control me, or who I went out with. Having dinner with Frost might remind him of that.

Or it might make the situation worse.

"I'm not as sweet as I look," Frost said. "If you could see inside my brain right now, you wouldn't think I'm even a tiny bit sweet. Most of my thoughts involve you naked, lying on your back while I stick my cock in your pussy. The other ones involve you on your knees, sucking my cock."

"That's better," I said approvingly. "I prefer not to think I'm corrupting you." I wasn't naïve enough to think I was leading him astray in any way. He'd had plenty of women to do that before he met me.

"If you did, I'd be there for it," he said. "I lost my virginity to my mother's best friend. I should say, former best friend. My mother wasn't impressed when she found out. Although, she took my best friend's virginity, so I think we're even. In case you're wondering, yes, my best friend was the son of her best friend. It was all very incestuous and shit." He grinned.

"That sounds like the...mother of all complications," I said, unable to resist the pun.

"It was," he agreed. "But I wouldn't have my little brother if it hadn't happened."

"And I thought my family was interesting," I said, half to myself. "Are you still friends with your best friend?"

"Yeah. I wouldn't let a little thing like knocking up my mother get between us," he said. "She's with some other guy now. My friend is married to a nice girl, living in the suburbs. They share custody of my little brother. He's an absolute terror, just like me." He grinned. "He's so cute he gets away with everything. All he has to do is smile and we give him whatever he wants."

"I bet you were like that when you were a kid," I observed.

"Exactly," he agreed. "I've always been good at using my charm and good looks to get my way."

He gave me a look that sent shivers of anticipation through me. He'd be a difficult one to say no to, that was for sure. Monday night was looking that much more enticing.

"What the fuck are you doing?"

I started as Storm stomped over to the table and stood beside us, glaring.

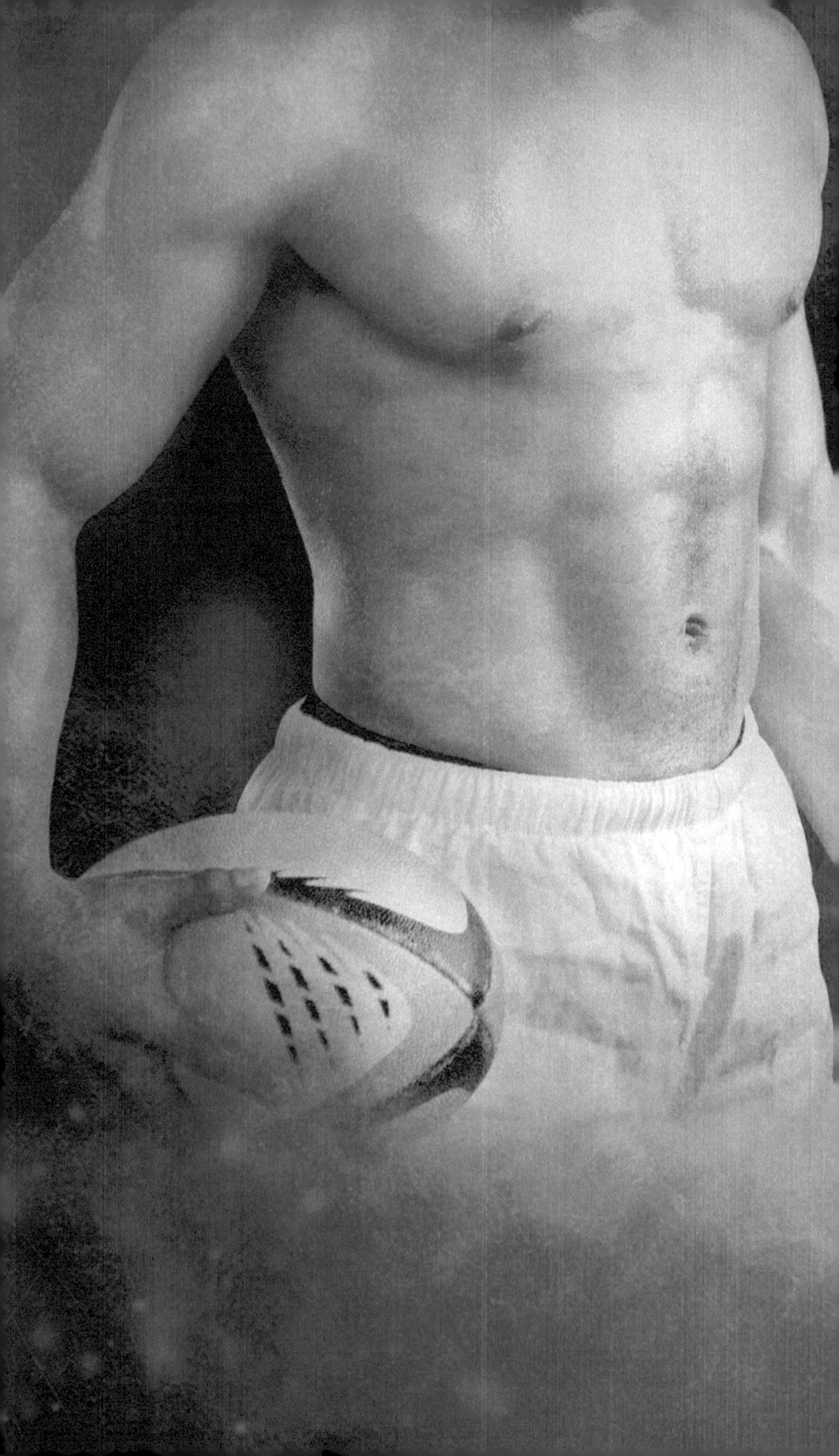

Chapter Ten

Chelsea

"Eating." I bit into my cupcake without giving Storm more than a passing glance. It was a good cupcake, perfectly moist.

Storm glared at Frost. "I asked you a question. What the fuck are you doing with her?"

"Also eating," Frost said easily. Only his eyes betrayed a hint of unease. "You're welcome to join us if you want, right Chelsea?"

"The more the merrier," I agreed.

Storm seemed like he'd sooner swallow his own tongue than sit and have a casual conversation over a sandwich. In spite of that, he grabbed the back of the chair beside us and dragged it out from under the table so the feet squeaked on the floor. He flopped down onto it and pulled it in closer.

"You know who she is?" he demanded, eyes narrowed at Frost, face slightly red.

"I do. I'm not quite sure you do," Frost said. "She's a doctor. She's doing—"

"I know exactly what she's doing here," Storm interrupted. "She wants to work here. If that's the case, she needs to avoid making waves." His gaze swivelled to me.

"I'm not the one getting all worked up," I pointed out. "You shouldn't do that either, it's bad for your blood pressure. You wouldn't want me to tell Coach you're not fit to play."

I kept my tone light, but there was no way in the world he'd miss the threat. It was as obvious as a football between the eyes.

Storm's jaw worked back and forth. "Don't fucking threaten me," he snarled.

"Then don't be a prick," I said. "I can eat lunch with whomever I want. So can Mr Frost here. He's been very hospitable." I didn't add 'unlike you,' it hung in the air for everyone to feel.

Storm's jaw worked harder. "I made myself clear the other night. Do you need a reminder?"

"No, but I think you need a reality check," I said. "You don't—"

He grabbed my wrist in his tight grip, fingers

pressing into my flesh. "I don't need a fucking reality check." He pulled me over closer to him so he could whisper in my ear. "I fucking own you. I. Fucking. Own. You. That's a fact. I decide who you eat lunch with."

"I think you should back off," Frost said coldly. "Chelsea gets to decide who she spends time with. If she doesn't want to spend time with you, she won't."

Storm released my wrist and sat with his forearms on the table. "It seems you both need an education." He closed his eyes and sucked in a breath through his nose. "Do you want him?" He looked over at me, eyes dark as thunderclouds. Darker.

Every muscle in my body was tense, matching his. Both of us were like bombs about to explode. I didn't want to draw too much attention to the conversation. Conflicts like this would get me kicked out before I even finished my placement. Something I suspected we were all acutely aware of, but no one more than me.

"We barely know each other," I said finally.

"You don't have to know someone to want to fuck them," Storm said. "Do you really think Frost here needs to know your likes and dislikes before he sticks his cock in you? He doesn't give a shit, do you Frosty?"

"I want to know her likes and dislikes," Frost said. After a moment, he admitted, "But I was interested before we exchanged a word."

"Exactly." Storm nodded. He looked back at me. "Do you want to fuck him?"

"I wouldn't be opposed to the idea," I said. I wanted to fuck Storm too, even while he was being a massive asshole. Burning with fury, he was hot enough to make my blood boil.

"What are your plans?" Storm directed the question to Frost.

"Dinner on Monday night," Frost said, after a long, anxious pause. "Unless Chelsea changed her mind."

"I didn't," I said. "We're definitely on for Monday." Whether Storm liked it or not.

Frost nodded and did his best not to flinch when Storm glared at him.

"Where?" Storm demanded.

"We haven't decided yet," I said. "Can you recommend somewhere nice?" I smiled sweetly.

Storm narrowed his eyes at me. "When you figure it out, tell me."

"Why should we?" I absently rubbed at my wrist where he grabbed me. Bruises were starting to form already. Other women would be horrified, but I was aroused. He'd left his mark on me. Physically and, to some extent, emotionally. Part of me was enjoying getting him worked up and irritated. Angry. Pushing his buttons could be dangerous, but I couldn't seem to resist.

"Because I fucking told you to," he snapped. "I want to know where my woman goes, who she sees and who she fucks."

"Your woman?" Frost asked. "Since when?"

"Since I said so," Storm said. "Since you were off fucking some other woman, remember?"

Frost slid his gaze away from both of us. "It was just... Before I got to know Chelsea."

"Everyone has a history," I said. "I'm willing to bet Storm does. He's not the friend who knocked up your mother, is he?"

Frost bit back a smile. "I don't think you could call us best friends, no. I wouldn't be surprised if he's fucked my mother though. They both get around."

Storm looked like he was about ready to break Frost's nose, but he didn't deny the other player's words. Maybe he had slept with his mother and maybe he hadn't. That was none of my business. The past was the past. For all I knew, I'd slept with both of their fathers.

"Wait a sec." Frost's brow creased in a deep V.

"What do you mean you want to know who Chelsea fucks?" Frost said, putting the conversation back to me. "Didn't you just imply she was yours?"

"I didn't imply anything," Storm said. "I stated a fact. Let me state another. She can go out with other men and screw their brains out, but I want to know about it."

"Are you expecting me to pay you so I can sleep with her?" Frost asked.

Storm lunged over the top of the table and grabbed a fistful of Frost's shirt before I could blink.

"I'm not a fucking pimp," he snarled. "If you pay to fuck her, that money goes to her. If she lets you fuck her for free, consider yourself lucky. Consider yourself lucky that I would let you fuck her, too."

Frost placed a hand on Storm's arm and pushed him away. "So you're saying she's yours, but you'll let me borrow her?"

Storm released the front of his shirt and sank back down in his chair. "That's precisely what I'm saying. Like if you borrowed my car, I'd want to know where you took it."

"Thank you for comparing me to your car," I said sarcastically.

He actually rolled his eyes. "My car is valuable.

One of my prized possessions." The look he gave me suggested he believed I was the other one.

I couldn't decide if he was hot as hell, or out of his mind. Possibly both. If I had any sense at all, I'd get up and walk away right now. Maybe I could get a placement with the Opal Springs Ghosts soccer team. Or the Sydney Devils rugby team. Somewhere far from Dusk Bay, and Storm Keller.

"This is so fucked up it's hot," Frost remarked. He adjusted himself again. "What if I decide she's mine too?"

I got the impression he wanted to ask what would happen if he also belonged to Storm.

Great, now I had the mental image of the big fullback bending him over the table in front of me, sliding his cock in and out of the prop's ass. That fantasy was almost hot enough to make me combust on the spot.

The look Storm gave Frost suggested he hadn't considered the possibility. He gave the matter some thought. Instead of telling Frost to fuck off, like I expected him to, he said, "I might be willing to share. A woman like her deserves to be taken care of. To be satisfied."

I didn't disagree with his words, but he was starting to sound like a Neanderthal. At any moment, he'd grab me by my hair and drag me off to his cave.

As far as I was aware, Neanderthal didn't actually live in caves, but he might. Honestly, he probably lived in the penthouse in Powell Tower, with a view over the ocean. The kind of place that was decorated with black marble, black leather and maybe a special room for the whips and chains.

"Can you not talk about me like I'm not here?" I said. "What if I decide to tell both of you to get lost?"

They both turned to me and gave me the same look. It wouldn't matter if I did, they'd made up their minds.

Storm shrugged. "You can try. You're not getting rid of us. I'm going to do everything I can to make sure you get that permanent...position here. So will Frosty."

Frost nodded vigourously. "Definitely. You deserve it. I know how hard you must have worked to become a doctor in the first place. Studying and working must have been exhausting."

"It was," I said carefully. "But I don't need either of you to do *anything* on my behalf. I got this far by working hard. I can get all the way by continuing to work hard."

The last thing I needed was for anyone to suggest

I was only hired because they pulled strings for me. I didn't need to be thinking that myself either. Up until now, I was the only one who could take any credit for my achievements. I didn't want that to change now.

"Of course you can." Storm reached over and started to run the tip of one of his fingers over the back of my wrist, sending tingles all the way through me. "But some of the guys are going to give you a hard time. We'll make sure they don't make trouble for you. If they do, I'll punch their fucking lights out. Then you can focus on what's important."

"I don't need you to punch anyone's lights out," I said, ending on a sigh. "You focus on your job and let me focus on mine. I don't want to see you in the infirmary with a broken hand, covered in someone else's blood."

Okay, maybe I did a little bit, but not because of me. If he was bloodied, with broken bones, it better be because he played harder than he ever had in his life. Because he smashed his opponents out there on the rugby field. Because he left his mark on them.

His fingers circled my wrist, his thumb rubbing over the bruises which were still darkening on my skin. His eyes darkened with them, his arousal obvious. He was turned on by them.

I had a feeling he wouldn't be satisfied until he'd left them everywhere on my body. Heaven help me, I'd let him do it too. I wanted him to cause me pain. I knew exactly where my limits were, and I knew he'd push me all the way to them. Maybe even beyond. I wanted that so much my pussy throbbed. My panties were absolutely ruined by now. I'd need to start bringing a spare pair or two to work if these were the conversations we were going to have.

"We'll text you when we've decided where we're eating." Evidently Frost was down for whatever Storm had in mind. Did he want to leave bruises on me too? His gaze dropped to my wrist, but I couldn't tell what he was thinking. I sensed he wanted to leave his mark on me, but in a different way. Something much darker than his sweet face hinted at. Maybe even something terrifying.

I knew beyond a shadow of a doubt it was too late for me to walk away, even if I wanted to. I probably should have, but I didn't.

I was in this as deep as they were, no matter the cost.

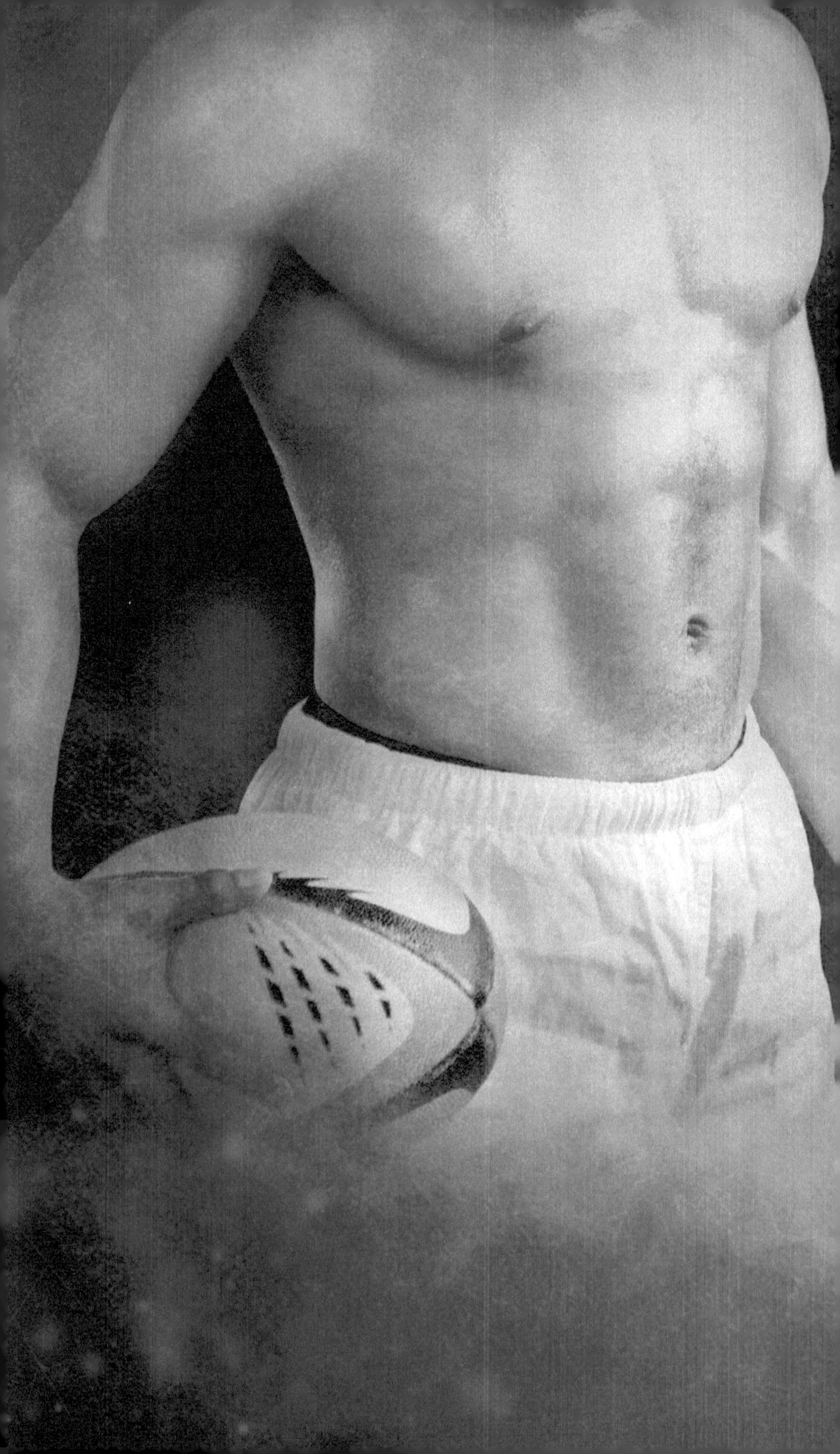

Chapter Eleven

Storm

Dallas was hovering around my locker when I stepped back into the locker room to get changed for training.

"You look like hell." I opened my locker and pulled out a pair of shorts.

"Thanks." The sarcastic response was bitten off by a clicking of teeth.

He was silent for long enough to make me look over at him again.

"If you've got something to say, spit it out," I said. "Otherwise, get ready for training before Coach gets on your back."

If Coach didn't, I would. The Smashers were going all the way to the premiership this year, even if I had to kick everyone's ass individually. On paper, we had what it took to step right over all the other teams on the table. We had the talent, we had the skills. What we didn't have was our shit together. That was unacceptable in my book.

"About the other night," Dallas' gravelly voice was low, each word reluctant. He dropped his gaze towards the floor. "That woman... The whore..."

He was lucky I didn't plant my fist right into his face. Chelsea was so much more than that. Smart, beautiful, and totally on board to let me use her the way I wanted to. Frost too.

Yeah, I'd seen the way he looked at some of the guys when he thought, hoped, no one else was looking. I would encourage him to explore that side of himself, and his attraction to Chelsea. But only her. If he so much as glanced at another woman, he'd be out. He was either all in with her and me, or he could fuck off.

"What about her?" I asked easily. "Seems to me you enjoyed her sucking you off."

I thoroughly enjoyed watching. Even the part where he staggered out the door. He'd done something he otherwise might not do, because I orchestrated it. Because I decided it would happen. Having that kind of control over the people around me was heady, arousing, addictive.

"What the hell *was* that?" Dallas looked up. "I don't pay for shit like that. I don't touch women like her."

I slammed my locker door hard enough to make him jump. "Yes, you do. I was there, I saw you do it. You were into it." He could deny it to himself, but facts were facts. He was hard for her and she got him off.

"What do you want?" He looked nervous. "Are you going to bribe me or something? If the club knew—"

I interrupted before he lost his shit. "I have no intention of telling the club. What we do on our time is our business. Don't read more into it then there was. You fucked her mouth, that was all. Don't get all worked up about having a good time."

I drew my head back and looked at him sideways. "That wasn't your first time, was it?"

He scoffed. "Of course not. I've fucked more women than you've had hot dinners. Just never a hooker."

Once again, I resisted the urge to punch him. "Then what's the problem? You didn't pay her a cent. I paid so you could entertain me by getting a blowjob. Mission accomplished."

"Do you know how fucked up that sounds?" He

didn't seem convinced. Like secretly he liked the idea. Watching or being watched, I couldn't tell.

"Just fucked up enough," I said. "I assume you'll be hurrying back to Flirts for more?"

I wanted to watch him fuck Chelsea before he knew she worked for the team. I wanted to see him slide his cock into her pussy, pound into her until he came inside her. Then I wanted to see the expression on his face when he entered the infirmary and saw her there.

I'd pay good money to be present for both.

"Definitely not," he said, his voice tight. His gaze didn't meet mine.

"But you want to," I guessed. "You want to see her again. Touch her. Screw her."

"So what if I do?" he said, seemingly louder than he intended. He drew back and lowered his voice. "I can't stop thinking about her. Her hot mouth on my dick. I keep thinking what it'd be like to have her swallow, you know?"

"She does seem to have that effect on people," I said. "I know for a fact she'd love to swallow down every drop of your cum."

"She said that?" He actually looked hopeful. Yeah, the guy was gone for her, whether he wanted to admit it or not.

"She didn't need to." I was enabling him and I didn't give a shit. "I saw it on her face. She would have taken anything you gave her."

She would, because I was going to tell her to. She'd fuck him because I wanted her to. Because the idea of it made my cock hard.

"I know where she'll be on Monday night," I added. "Away from Flirts. I know she'll be receptive to spending more time with both of us."

"Both of us," Dallas echoed. His eyes were dark with lust.

"Both, or you're out," I said, as blunt with him as I was with Frost. This happened under my terms or not at all.

He looked conflicted, torn between doing what I said and his need for her. Finally, he nodded. "Fine, I'm in. As long as she's okay with that."

"She will be," I said firmly. She would be, because I wanted her to be. If she accepted the situation, it would be easier on her, but she'd do what I said either way. Her independence was cute, but her obedience— That would be even better.

"I'll text you the details," I said. "Don't be late, or I might change my mind."

"I won't be," he said quickly.

I believed him. He knew something strange,

maybe unsavoury, was up, but he wouldn't miss this opportunity. There was a darkness in him that was waiting to be unleashed. The same as there was in Frost and in me. Chelsea would discover the full extent of that, when we used her body.

"You two are intense over here," Frost remarked. "Everything okay?"

If he was anyone else, I would have told him to piss off. If it wasn't for his involvement with Chelsea, and the fact he was one of the genuinely nice guys on the team, I would have. Yeah, there was darkness in him, but there was also innocence I was looking forward to unravelling. An inner animal that only came out on the field. I wanted to help him to let it out in other areas of his life.

"I was just inviting Dallas out with us on Monday night," I said. "For the after-dinner entertainment."

Frost blinked at me, then at Dallas. "This is getting cosy." He didn't immediately object. If anything, he seemed interested in exploring an unexpected opportunity. Maybe he wanted to suck Dallas off too. If that was the case, I'd do what I could to nudge them toward each other. I suspected Chelsea would enjoy watching them fuck each other. I knew I would.

"You said both," Dallas said to me.

"I did, didn't I," I said unapologetically. "I meant all of us. One at a time, or maybe all at once. I haven't decided yet."

"Who said you get to decide?" Frost didn't look angry, he looked wary. Like he was worried I'd mess this up for him. That maybe I'd exclude him. The expression in his eyes held a hint of defiance, but something else. Fear. He was scared that I'd throw a bomb at the budding relationship between him and Chelsea, and blow it all to kingdom come.

I could do exactly that, but I wouldn't. Whatever it was between them, I wanted to nurture it. Just like I wanted to nurture my quickly growing bond with the beautiful doctor.

"I did," I said finally. "I've been playing for the team longer than anyone else and I met her first. If you're going to argue, then you can fuck off."

"Chelsea and I made plans—" Frost started.

"And I'm letting you keep them," I said evenly. "This is how it is. We all agreed to it. And now Dallas is a part of it. End of story." I turned from both of them to change my shorts.

"You're an asshole," Frost said, his voice deep and low.

I glanced back.

His gaze bore into me, dark with lust. "This shouldn't be hot."

"Maybe you like being told what to do." I kept my own voice low. "Maybe I should tell you to suck my cock."

Saying the words out loud made my balls ache. If I didn't bury my cock in Chelsea soon, I was going to blow my top. Getting myself off in the shower every morning was not enough. I needed to lose myself in her, spill my cum into her body and claim her. I needed it so badly it hurt. Ached. I liked to take a little pain, as well as inflicting it, but even I had my limits.

His Adam's apple bobbed and his gaze dropped toward my groin. He swiped his tongue over his lips.

"We're supposed to be getting ready for training," Dallas said. His voice was as heavy as ours. Caught up in the vibe. The tent in his pants backed that up.

"Maybe I should tell Frosty to suck your cock?"

Would they do it? They wanted to, that was obvious, but wanting to do something and actually doing it weren't the same thing. This was something I couldn't force, not yet. But I'd given them something to think about. They'd probably jerk off later, the thought embedded in their minds. In their heated blood.

"What are you three pricks doing over there?" Atlas called out from the other side of the locker room.

His words broke the tension, shattering the moment for now.

"They're probably planning to have a unicorn-themed sleepover party," Jay said, as if that was some kind of epic burn.

Ramsey laugh-grunted from where he sat in the corner.

"I think they're cut up about not being invited," I said loudly. "I can tell Jay is gutted to miss out on a cake shaped like a unicorn."

What kind of shit was this guy projecting, exactly? He clearly had unresolved childhood issues he should be discussing with his therapist. Personally, I felt sorry for any kid who missed out on a party with a unicorn theme. Not that I had one, but I had friends who did and I might have gone to one or two of them. Clearly, Jay hadn't.

"Fuck off," Jay snapped.

"What an articulate comeback," I said sarcastically. "Let me guess, he never got invited to parties as a kid." That was sad, but not surprising. Jay was a sullen asshole, with a chip on his shoulder and his head up his ass. If he wasn't such a good rugby player, I'd have no respect for him at all. Just like he had none for me.

"I got invited to plenty," he snarled. "Every fucking weekend. None with any unicorn shit." Yeah, he definitely had issues.

I smirked. I'd sooner invite them to have a unicorn sleepover than spend time with Chelsea. The fact she'd have to treat them sooner or later made me see red. The fact there was nothing I could do about it made me angrier still.

I wanted to control her life and her body, but I wouldn't stop her from doing her job. I needed her to want me, not resent me. Asking her to stop being a doctor would be like her asking me to give up rugby. That was not going to happen.

"All right, guys," Coach Stanley shouted. "Let's get out there."

I ignored Jay and Atlas and trotted out the door and onto the field.

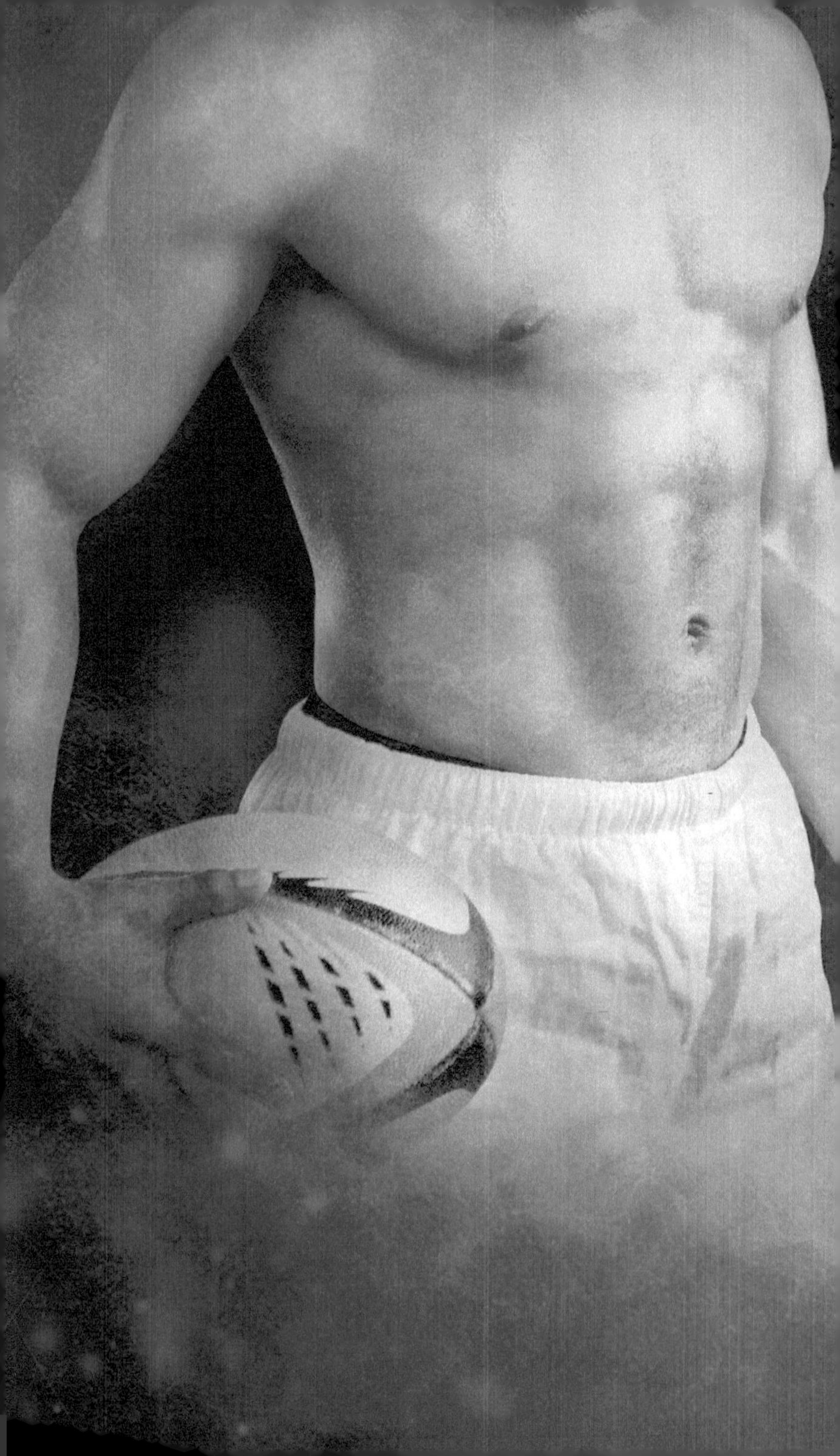

Chapter Twelve

Chelsea

"I guess I was wrong. I got the feeling Storm would tag along." I'd glanced around the restaurant, taking in the heavy wooden tables, high backed chairs and sparkling view over Dusk Bay. Two tables over, a couple of the Dusk Bay Demons sat with a cute redhead, pretending not to notice when she stole chips from their plates.

Near the window, a couple of members of Ice Blue Roses, the rock band, had a quiet, but heated conversation. The rumour the bass player had a falling out with the rest of the band might be true after all.

Servers bustled around, quick and efficient, but trying to be non-intrusive.

So far, I saw no sign of the big fullback.

"I think he wanted to, but he decided to leave us alone so we could eat," Frost said.

Like he had in the stadium cafeteria the other day, he pulled out a chair and waited for me to sit.

I still gave him a look, but lowered myself into the chair and got comfortable. "How do you feel about this arrangement?"

"I like the idea of having dinner with you." He settled into the chair beside me and handed me a menu.

I took it and resisted the urge to swat him on the arm with the leather bound wine list. "I meant the rest of it. The whole 'him thinking he owns me,' thing." My nipples hardened and ached as the words left my lips. The increased blood flow through my whole body made my clit throb.

"Honestly, I think it's hot," Frost said frankly. "He's always been intense and possessive of the team, but I've never seen him like that about another person. He must have it bad for you." He looked down at his menu like he was averting his gaze.

"I'm not sure if he cares about me or just likes to boss me around," I said. "What is he like to play with?" My choice of words was deliberate.

Frost swallowed. "I don't—" He cleared his throat. "Right, you mean rugby. He's very dedicated.

Very skilled. He's one of the best fullbacks in the country, if not the world. He's one of the most driven people I ever met. When he decides he wants something, he goes after it. On the field and off."

"I guessed that about him," I said. "He's a lot like me in that respect. What about you? Do you go after what you want?"

He looked at me through lashes so long they should probably be illegal. "Yeah, I do. But I... I don't always get it. Not in the way I want to, anyway."

"You don't want to play for the Smashers?" I asked.

Sometimes players had to take whatever club would have them. Even high-profile players didn't always get their way.

"I do," he said quickly. "I've always wanted to play international. For Australia. The older I get, the less likely it seems. It gets harder every year; the talent I'm up against is next level."

"There's no reason why you can't still be chosen," I said. "You're at the peak of your fitness. I've watched you play, you're incredible. Your instincts on the field never let you down."

He glanced back down at the menu again. "Yeah, I dunno. I feel like I'm not seen past the other guys."

"Are we still talking about rugby?" I asked gently. I placed a hand on his firm thigh.

"Not just that," he agreed. "But enough about me. How was your first week with the team?"

"Amazing," I said. "Exhausting. Rewarding. I look forward to meeting the rest of the players." So far, I'd spent more time doing paperwork than treating anyone, but that was to be expected.

He scratched the side of his head. "I hope you don't forget me when you do."

"How could I forget you?" I moved my hand up his thigh, towards his groin. "You're the sweet one, remember?"

"My thoughts aren't sweet right now," he warned. "If you knew what I was really like, you might run out the door."

"And yet, a statement like that intrigues me," I said. "I'm a big believer in people being their authentic selves."

"I want to show you that side of me," he said softly. "Will you let me?" He looked at me earnestly, as though half hoping I'd refuse, but desperate for me to agree.

I only took a moment to think about it. Curiosity quickly overruled any caution I should have had. "Yes, I'll let you. Should we eat first?"

He glanced around like he forgot where we were, shook his head to remind himself. "Yes, we should eat and... And drink." The words were loaded, spiking my curiosity further.

He gestured for the server to take our orders and we handed over our menus.

"I hope you like the food. I've been here lots of times and I think it's really good." He looked anxious now, nervous.

"I'm sure it's delicious," I said. "Will you excuse me for a moment? I need to go to the ladies room."

He nodded again and rose to help me with my chair. For some reason, he looked relieved. Was my company that tedious? No, it was something else. Something he had in mind.

In spite of that, I half-expected him to be gone when I got back, but he wasn't. He was sitting at our table, hands in his lap. The server dropped off our meals and drinks while I was in the bathroom.

"This looks so good." I waved him down when he started to stand to help me sit. "Let's dig in."

"Yes," he said quickly. He picked up his fork and stabbed it into a meatball. "Can I tell you something?"

"Sure." I cut open a ravioli and started to eat.

"I can't stop thinking about you," he said. "You're

beautiful and smart. And sexy. I've never met anyone like you."

"To be honest, I can't stop thinking about you too," I said. And Storm as well, but the fullback could easily have overpowered my thoughts with his personality. He hadn't, not entirely. I was intrigued by Frost. By the edge of darkness that flitted across his expression every now and again. I wanted to dig underneath that sweet exterior to find out what was underneath.

I didn't know who had looked past him to everyone else, to *anyone* else, because I couldn't look away. The more time I spent with him, the more I wanted to get to know him. To touch him. To taste him. I wasn't sure who would be claiming who. Maybe we'd claim each other. Maybe I could be as possessive of him as Storm was of me.

"You can't?" He looked genuinely surprised.

"I really can't," I assured him. "I feel drawn to you. I don't think I could stop myself if I wanted to, which I don't. You have a lot to offer, I can tell."

"I do," he said easily. "I want to give all of it to you. Everything." He watched me carefully as I picked up my wine. His expression was anxious, like he was invested in me taking a drink. Had he done something to it?

His tongue swiped over his lower lip. "Drink your wine," he said softly. "It'll help to relax you."

He'd slipped something into my drink.

"How relaxed?" I asked carefully.

"Just the right amount," he assured me. "Take a drink."

I lifted the wine to my lips and took a big sip.

He smiled in relief. "Good girl." He concentrated on finishing his dinner and sipping light beer, while watching me drink the rest of my wine.

"This was beautiful," I said. "The food was so good. And the company is excellent."

He grinned. "I'll pay while you... Finish your drink."

"I can pay for myself," I protested. I tried to stifle a yawn, but I could barely raise my arm to put my hand over my mouth.

He was looking at me expectantly, his head cocked.

"What did you..." I blinked, the movement slower than usual. Sluggish. More than relaxed.

"Nothing that'll hurt you," he said quickly. "I told you I wanted to show you the real me. I have a... preference. Don't worry, you'll be awake. I want you aware of everything I'm going to do to you."

He slipped me something to incapacitate me, not

just relax me. I could have panicked, but instead I surrendered to whatever he gave me. It wasn't like I had much of a choice. Soon, I'd be unable to move.

"Come on, before it kicks in." He stood and took my hand to pull me to my feet.

I made it to the door before my legs started to fold underneath me. He lowered his shoulder and threw me over it, his arms wrapped around my legs.

I couldn't run, couldn't scream if I wanted to. All I could do was dangle over his shoulder while he carried me to his car and lowered me into the back seat.

"This is the real me," he whispered. "I want to be in complete control of you. I'm going to fuck you and you're going to lie there and let me."

I looked up at his face and blinked.

I was right, there was darkness in him. He'd asked to show this side of himself to me, and I agreed. I drank the laced wine, knowing what was coming. Intrigued by both the expression on his face and my own imagination. Wanting to completely let go and give him everything he needed. Let him act out his darkest fantasies with me.

I was completely at his mercy and there was nothing I could do about it. I couldn't protest or back out now. I was all the way in and he soon would be. My clit throbbed, aroused beyond belief.

He pushed my skirt up to my waist, pulled the gusset of my panties aside and slipped his fingers inside me. "You're nice and wet. Perfect. Exactly how I need you." Fascinated, he toyed with the piercing in the hood of my clit, making my whole body tingle. "So fucking pretty."

He pulled his fingers out of me, opened the front of his jeans and pushed them down his hips far enough to let his erection bob free. He straddled me before notching the tip of his cock inside my pussy.

"I'm going to enjoy this so much," he whispered. "All I've wanted to do since I met you was take you. To use your body in the way it was intended. You were made to give me pleasure. Made to take my cock. Made to take my cum. I'm going to give all of it to you. And you're going to take all of it."

Slowly, he pushed himself all the way inside me. All the way to his balls.

My muscles wanted to tense, but I was too relaxed to do anything but welcome him into me. Letting his wide, thick length slide unimpeded into my wet heat.

His cock was so big he filled me in a way I'd never been before.

I couldn't move, but I could feel. I felt every thrust as he slid out of me and slammed back in. He propped himself on his elbows and pounded into me with even strokes. All the while, he kept his eyes on me, a smile on the corners of his lips.

"Now you're mine," he whispered. "In every way." He pulled down the front of my shirt and the cup of my bra, dipped his head to lick at one of my nipples, then drew it in between his lips to suck. "Delicious. You probably think this is fucked up. Maybe it is. Taking a woman who can't fight back…"

He shook his head. "You have no idea how much I needed this. How many times I've fantasised. I thought about holding you down, but it wasn't enough. I needed to know I could take what I wanted and you couldn't stop me. I needed to be sure."

He half-closed his eyes and fucked me faster. "You feel so good. You like having my cock inside you, don't you?"

I managed a slight sound in the back of my throat, a low moan. Everything about this was fucked up, but at the same time I wanted to keep living out his fantasy. Knowing he had complete control of my body was arousing.

If I could, I would have rolled my hips, matching

each of his thrusts. I would have arched my back and cried out when I came, right there on the back seat of his car. I would have told him not to stop, not ever. I could have lain there for hours while he slid in and out of me, using me.

"I'm going to come inside you," he whispered.

I managed to move my lips and gasp out one word, "Please."

It wasn't a plea for him to stop. Anything but. I wanted him to spill himself inside my body. I wanted him to claim me. I wanted him to own me. I gave myself over to him fully. I wasn't Chelsea right now, I was his fuck toy. His to do with whatever he wanted.

And I'd let him do it again. His power over me was an aphrodisiac. He was right, he wasn't sweet, and I wouldn't want to change that. This darker side of him was hotter than hell.

"Fuck," he whispered before he let go. He pounded into me harder before falling still and coming hard, as deep inside me as he could go. Spilling every drop of his release.

He sagged over me, puffing lightly before getting his breath back. "You're everything," he whispered.

"What the fuck?" Storm's voice came from just outside the car.

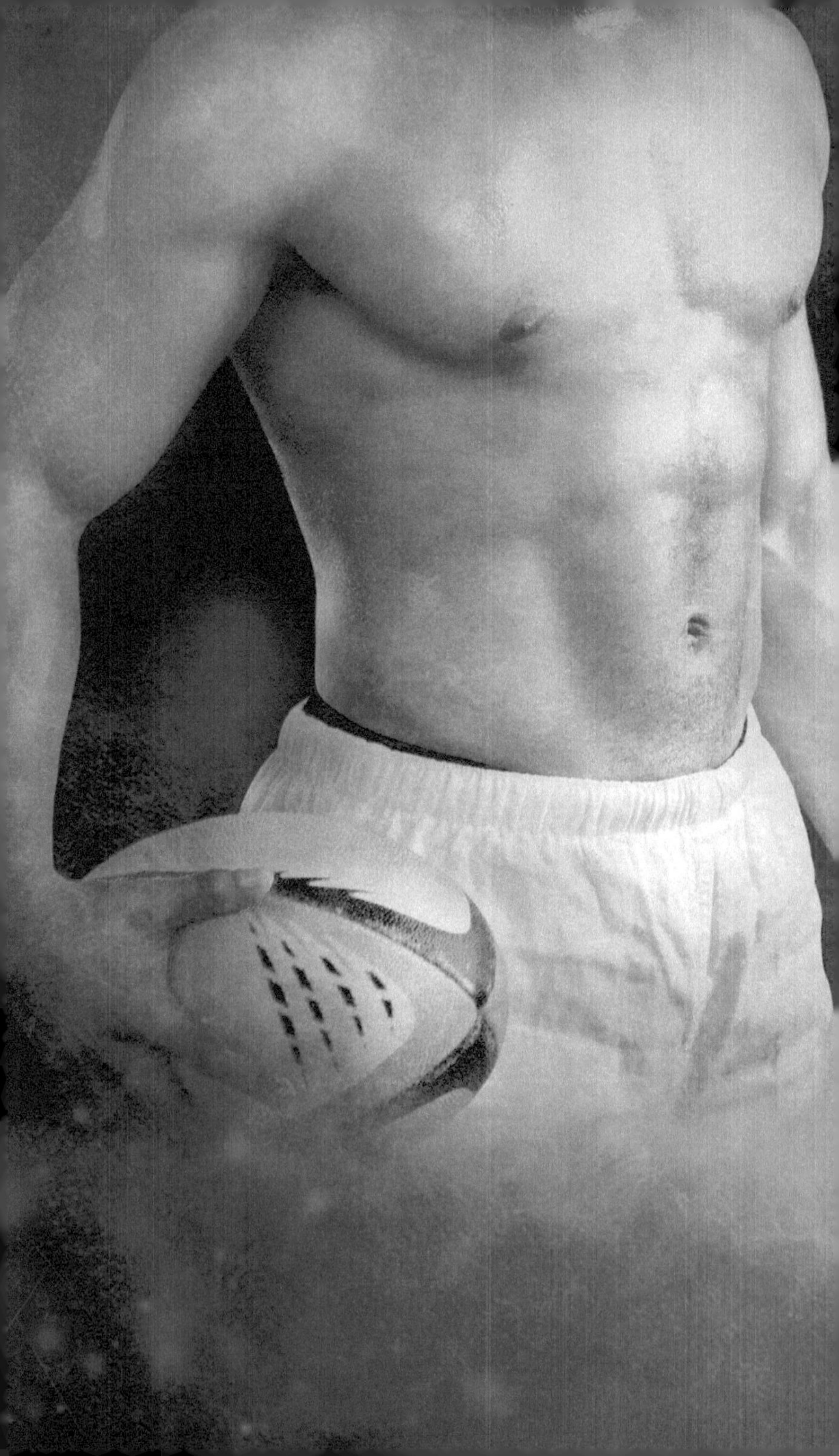

Chapter Thirteen

Chelsea

I TRIED TO TURN MY HEAD, BUT I BARELY managed more than a millimetre. I was able to move my lips, slightly, and my toes. Whatever Frost slipped me—I had a reasonably good idea of what must have been a small dose and was gradually wearing off.

Part of me wished it would hurry up. At the same time, I could have lain here, just like this, for longer. Storm and Frost could have taken turns, fucking me while I could do nothing but let them use me.

"Hey," Frost greeted Storm, his expression tentative, but defiant.

"What did you do to her?" Storm scowled down at me.

"Nothing she didn't want." Frost slid out of me and pulled his pants back into place.

Storm ignored him. "Chelsea?"

I looked back at him, barely blinking.

He grabbed Frost by the back of his shirt and pulled him out of the car. He dumped him hard on the concrete before reaching for me. Hand tight on my wrist, he pulled until I was close enough for him to lift out of the back seat.

It wasn't until I was in his arms that I saw Dallas hovering a couple of metres back. He scowled at Frost like he might grab him and bash the back of his head into the side of his own car.

"What did he do?" Storm's voice was surprisingly gentle, but laced with fury. He might rip Frost's face off if he didn't get some answers soon.

"Like I said, nothing she didn't want me to." Frost placed his hands on the side of the car behind him and pushed himself to his feet. "You don't think I'd fucking hurt her, do you?"

"Look at her," Storm demanded. "She can barely fucking move. You drugged her, then fucked her." His tone was dangerous now. His fury made his face red. He clearly assumed I hadn't consented to what Frost did to me. Did he really think Frost would force himself on me? Was Frost really the kind of guy who'd do that?

Evidently, Storm and Dallas thought so.

"She knew what she was taking," Frost said, struggling to keep his voice even. "She let me do it. She wanted to."

"She wanted to be helpless?" Storm asked. "That's—" He shook his head, but doubt had started to settle in his mind. He didn't want to believe Frost would rape me, but he wasn't completely convinced. "I don't have time for this. I'm getting her out of here. I'll deal with your sorry ass later."

Frost looked like he wanted to argue, but finally he sagged. "She drove her own car. It's over there." He nodded towards my little yellow hatchback before reaching into his car for my bag and phone. He shoved both at Dallas and stepped back, like the other man might literally bite his head off.

Dallas pulled out my keys and unlocked my car. He opened the door and let Storm place me inside. "Where are you taking her?"

"My place." Storm clicked my seatbelt into place and took the keys from Dallas. "Fun's over, go home."

Dallas shot Frost a caustic glare, but nodded and stalked off to his own car. His whole body was stiff, anger and frustration radiating off him. Was he frustrated at Frost, Storm, or me? I wasn't sure. That was a matter for tomorrow, not tonight.

"I wouldn't do anything to hurt her," Frost called out before Storm closed the door and started the engine.

"I should run the prick over," Storm muttered before putting the car in reverse and backing out of the parking space.

I managed a slight sound of disagreement in the back of my throat. The fact Storm wasn't punching the shit out of Frost as we spoke suggested he had some idea of the truth. Maybe he didn't want to accept it yet, but he knew.

He sighed. "I shouldn't have let him take you out. If I knew what he'd do, I wouldn't have. Pulling shit like this in a public place is bullshit."

So that was what had him so angry.

He glanced over at me. "Anyone could have walked up. They could have used you. Without your consent, or mine."

I couldn't tell which would have annoyed him more. Me being raped, or anyone touching me without his permission.

I knew which one of those bothered *me* more.

I managed a sound of annoyance.

He chuckled. "Did I piss you off? You know the

score. If anyone touches you without your consent *and* mine, I'll rearrange their fucking face."

He fell silent and focused on driving, moving the car through the light traffic.

"You could have had some kind of reaction to what he gave you," Storm said finally.

I could move my fingers now. The drug was wearing off more rapidly. I tried again to speak. "I didn't," I managed to whisper.

"Lucky for him, because he'd be floating in the middle of the bay right now if you had." He pulled into the driveway and waited for the door leading to the undercover parking in Powell Tower to open.

"I'm fine." His overprotectiveness was starting to grate on my nerves. "You could take me home."

I could use a shower and some time to decompress, and for the drug to wear off fully. Maybe a coffee strong enough to drive the rest of it away, out of my system. Or at least, let it feel like it was doing that. At this point, nothing I could take would make it leave my bloodstream quicker. Nothing but time.

"I'm not letting you out of my sight until the shit in your system is gone." He backed my little hatchback into a parking space and turned off the engine. Footsteps heavy on the concrete, he hurried around to my side and started to lift me out of the car.

I tried to protest, but my whole body was weighed down with lead. I had no choice but to let him carry me all the way up to his apartment.

Shoving the door open with his back, he carried me into his bedroom. Carefully, as if I might break, he placed me down on his bed and sat beside me. "You look good in my bed."

I twitched my eyebrows at him. "You didn't need to do this."

"Of course I did." He brushed hair back off my forehead. "I take care of what's mine."

He pulled off my shoes and tossed them aside on the floor. "You really took whatever he gave you on purpose?"

"I did," I agreed. "I swallowed it all down. Let him live out his fantasy. As far as kinks go, his is harmless fun."

Storm grunted. "It's fucked up."

"You don't have any fucked up fantasies?" I asked. Some might argue that paying me to fuck another man was fucked up.

"Of course I do," he said. "They just don't involve making you helpless."

I tried to sit up, but my body still wouldn't comply. "Some men get off on fucking people while they're asleep. Or completely unconscious. I was awake and aware."

"Would you let him fuck you while you're unconscious?" Storm frowned.

"Maybe," I said. "I don't know if that's what he's into."

He chewed on that for a few moments. "I knew there was something screwy about him. I wonder how he'd feel about being so helpless."

"That might be his ultimate fantasy," I said. If Storm and Frost wanted to act that out, I wanted to watch. "What's yours?"

He worked his jaw back and forth until I thought he might not tell me. Finally, he said, "You know I like to be in control."

"I might have noticed that," I teased lightly.

"Don't make me spank your ass," he growled playfully.

"Don't threaten me with a good time," I retorted. "What kind of control do you want over me? The same as Frost?"

He took a moment to respond. When I thought he might change the subject, he finally said, "No, I want you to be able to fight back. I want you to struggle and scream, and I want to take you while you do it. But I want you to let me." He averted his gaze, uncomfortable with having admitted to something dark. Something I might judge him for. Something that set my blood on fire like a lit match on petrol.

"Rape fantasy is a relatively common kink," I said. It was one of mine. "With or without drugs involved. I want to explore that with you." I waited until he turned his face back to me before adding, "I like it when my partners get rough."

He exhaled a ragged breath and moved to lean against the pillows beside me. "That was why you took what Frost gave you? You like to let men take control when they fuck you?"

"Depending on the man, yes," I said. "But only then. Not at work, or outside the bedroom." I waited for him to disagree and I wasn't disappointed.

"What you do at work is totally within your control," he said slowly. "But I'm going to keep a closer eye on the rest of your time. Now you're here, you can stay."

"I have a perfectly good apartment of my own," I argued. I wasn't surprised he suggested it though, especially after tonight. Of course he'd want to keep me close.

"Rent it out," he said simply. "I'll organise a removalist in the morning."

"No," I said firmly. "Starting with the fact we barely know each other, and ending with the fact I'm still on placement. If the Smashers find out I'm living with you, they'll terminate the rest of it. My chance to work for the team will be gone forever. I may never work for another team either. I'm not giving that up." He could fight me on this, but he wouldn't win, because I was right.

His jaw was set, and I thought he might argue anyway, but he eventually nodded. "When your placement is over and the team hires you, you'll live here."

"Maybe I will, and maybe I won't," I said. "I'm not going to think about it until my placement is finished. I need to focus on that, and you need to focus on the season. If you're going to let me be a distraction, I'll walk away right now."

"Not letting you walk away," he said. "You won't distract me as long as you do what I tell you to do. I'll let you keep living at your place for now. We'll talk about the rest later. In the meantime, I'll wash Frost's cum off your pussy."

"I'm going to see him again," I said before Storm scooped me up and carried me to his bathroom.

"We'll see," was all he said before he sat me down beside the bath.

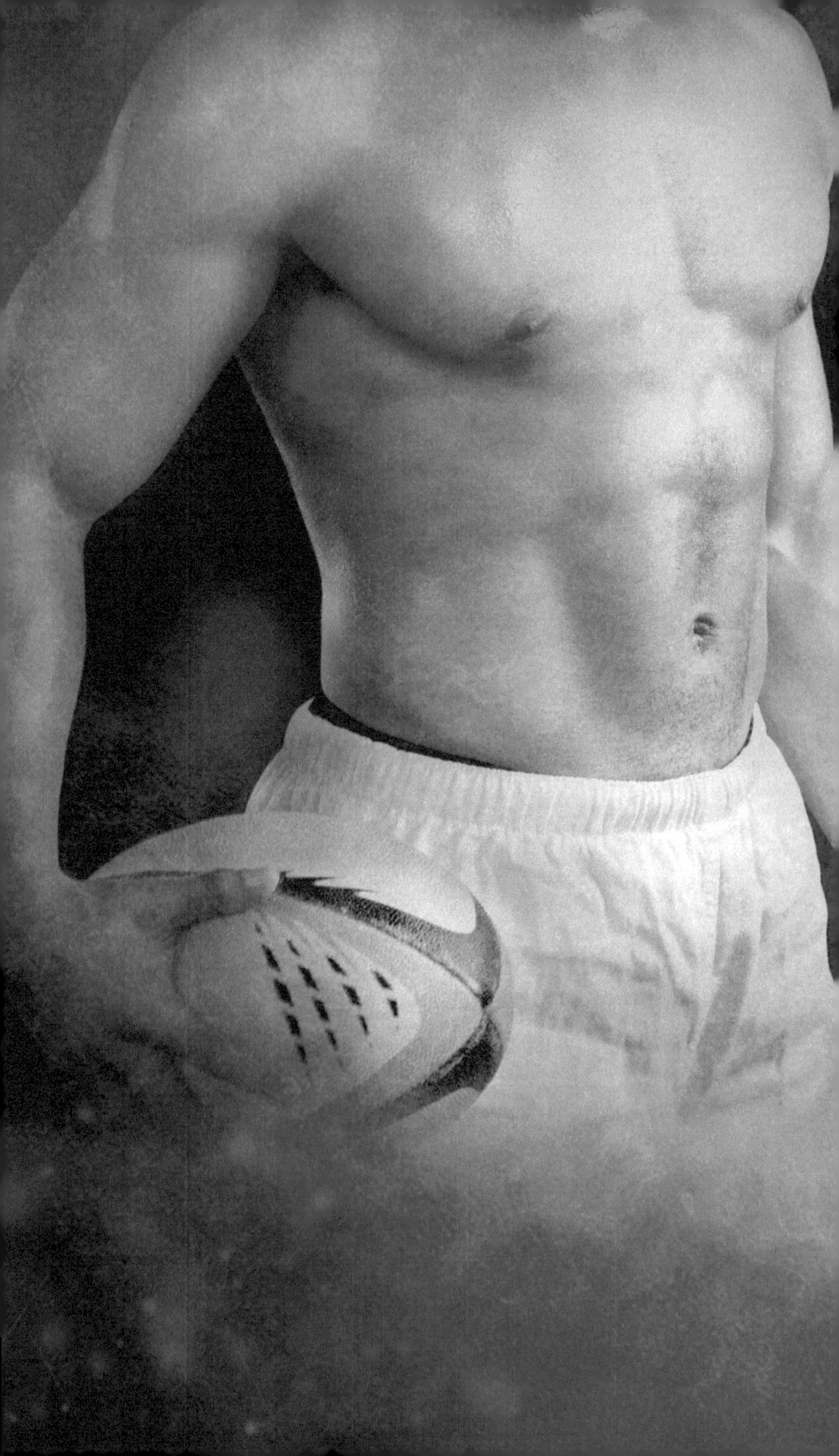

Chapter Fourteen

Chelsea

I woke up feeling warm, but tired.

On the upside, I could move now. Sort of. Storm lay beside me, one arm draped over my stomach. He'd helped me take a quick bath before dressing me in a pair of his track pants and a Smashers T-shirt. Both were too big for me, but comfortable enough.

He started to stir. "Morning." He was dressed in a pair of grey track pants which did nothing to hide his morning arousal.

"Hi." I pushed myself until I was sitting up and swiped stray hair off my cheek. I grabbed my phone from where he'd put it on the table beside the bed and looked at the time. I didn't start work for a couple of hours, thank fuck. Oversleeping and being late would not be a good look.

"I should get going." I yawned and stretched, enjoying having my full range of motion again.

"Not yet." Storm rolled over, pushed me back down and straddled my legs. He grabbed my wrists and held them up above my head. "We have some unfinished business to attend to."

"Do we?" I asked sweetly. "I thought we sorted out everything last night." As if I didn't know exactly what he had in mind.

"We came to an understanding," he agreed. "But my cock remains unsatisfied. I promised him we'd fuck you last night and that didn't happen."

"Because you decided to bring me back here." I met his gaze. "You were a gentleman, instead of taking me in the back of Frost's car like you could have."

He pressed his growing erection into the side of my leg. "I was tempted. Your pussy was right there, begging to be fucked." He rocked his cock against me. "I could have pushed down my jeans, climbed on top of you and slammed right on into you."

"Why didn't you?" I asked. "I couldn't have done anything to stop you."

He held my wrists with one hand while sliding the other up the front of my T-shirt and over my hardened nipples. "I should have. You belong to me.

I could have shown you then and there." He pinched one of my nipples hard.

"Yes, you could have." The pain from the pinch shot through me, making my clit throb. "You could have done whatever you wanted and I would have just laid there and taken everything you gave me."

He pinched my other nipple. "Next time, I will."

He wouldn't have done it last night, knowing there was no way I could consent to him touching me. But this conversation? He was taking this as my consent if the situation ever arose again. Unless I told him otherwise, he'd fuck me while I was drugged and helpless.

He pushed up the front of my T-shirt and scooted down to lick and suck first one nipple, then the other. "These are mine. Both of them. They belong to me."

He moved slowly down my body until he reached the waistband of my track pants. He let go of my wrists and dragged the pants down to my ankles and off over my feet.

I pulled off the T-shirt and let it join the track pants on the floor beside the bed. "Are you going to fuck me now?"

His gaze wandered up and down my body, eyes dark with hunger. "Yes, I'm going to fuck you." He rolled over and pulled a pair of handcuffs out of the drawer in the table beside him. He took my wrists again and cuffed me to the head of his bed.

"Much better."

He pried my legs apart with his hands, opening me out to him. He slid his thick fingers slowly up and down my thighs before tracing circles over my clit with the pad of his thumb.

"This belongs to me too. I own this pussy."

"You think so?" I asked teasingly.

He raised an eyebrow at me before leaning over to pull something else out of the drawer. A long strip of fabric. He pressed it between my lips and tied the ends around behind my head. "Now you can't talk back."

I gave a short laugh around the gag and let my eyes smile at him.

"If that's how you want to play it." He grabbed my hips and rolled me over onto my stomach. He brought his hand down to slap my ass hard enough to bring tears to my eyes. The sting of pain made me wetter than hell.

He slapped me again, harder this time, before switching to the other cheek.

"They look perfect with my handprint on them," he said. He pinched my ass a couple of times, hard enough to leave bruises. "I want you to think about me every time you sit down. I want you to remember the way you talked back to me. A few bruises and you might learn to behave yourself."

He pushed my legs open and ran the side of his knuckles up and down my pussy, grazing my clit. "This piercing makes you more sensitive, doesn't it?"

I made a sound of agreement through the gag. Every time he touched my clit, the piercing bobbed against it, arousing me more and more.

"Are you going to be good and come for me, or do I have to smack you again?"

How did I answer that question? Either way, I was winning. With his fingers rubbing me, more determined now, I couldn't keep myself from coming. The world exploded around me, into a thousand twinkling lights. I arched my back and cried out through the gag. All I knew for at least a minute, was pure, lasting bliss. A place I didn't want to come back from.

I barely started to come down when he straddled my legs and positioned his cock outside my entrance.

"I've been waiting too long for this," he whispered. Slowly, centimetre by centimetre, he pushed himself into me from behind. He took his time, savouring every moment and giving my muscles time to get used to his girth. He was bigger than Frost. Big enough that I wasn't sure I'd be able to take all of him, until he was seated inside to his balls.

"Fucking hell, you feel good," he groaned. "Just like I knew you would. How many men have seen this pussy? Hundreds? Thousands? But I'm the one who gets to fuck you right now. I'm the one who gets to claim you and your body. I'm the one who gets to own you."

He was still for a couple of minutes before starting to thrust slowly, taking his time. He slid all the way out me, and all the way back in, over and over as if he had all day to fuck me thoroughly. Big hands gripping my hips, he drove in over and over.

When I thought he was about to come, he pulled out and rolled me over onto my back. He pulled my legs up over his shoulders and pushed back into me. This time, when he slammed into me, he touched me all the way through, hard, painful, perfect.

His thrusts were firmer now, relentlessly pounding, giving me everything he had. Making me take all of him. Holding nothing back.

"Look at me," he ordered.

I looked up, locking my eyes on him. Watching the big fullback as he fucked me. His whole body was muscular, chiselled, glorious. Every thrust made me aroused again, pushing me quickly towards the edge of the cliff.

"Keep your eyes on me," he said. "I want you to watch me come inside you. You're going to take everything I give you and you're going to be grateful for it. Understood?"

He grabbed the side of the gag and tugged it down, out of my mouth. "Understood?"

"I understand," I said. "Give me everything. Come inside me."

I thought he might put the gag back in place, but instead he thrust harder until he went still, his orgasm making him groan and grind into me.

At the same time, I came again, muscles tightening around his throbbing cock. I forced myself to keep my eyes locked on him while blood raced around my body, drowning me in a wave of pleasure.

"Storm!" I cried out. "Oh, God, yes. Yes, yes, yes."

"That's it, come for me," he said, his voice tight with tension before it started to ebb away. "Take my cum."

The second orgasm was more intense than the first, lasting longer and taking my breath for several seconds.

Finally, reluctantly, I came back down to earth.

He slid out of me, lowered my legs from his shoulders, but kept my knees apart, his eyes on my pussy. "I can see my cum inside you. So fucking beautiful."

He lowered his mouth to my entrance and licked me clean of his release. "I wish I could bottle the taste of your pussy. I'd make a fucking fortune."

He scooted up the bed and pressed his mouth to mine. "Taste yourself."

I kissed him, and licked his lips, savouring the taste of both of our releases. "Delicious."

"Later, we'll talk about getting rough," he said. "Unless you want me to surprise you."

"Surprise me," I said after a few moments of careful thought. "I'll be ready."

I was surprised he wanted to give me the choice. He'd given me every indication he was aware of the need for consent, but he'd push those boundaries as far out as they'd go. I suspected he was like this in all areas of his life. Always testing the borders around him and seeing where they might be stretched, or broken.

He didn't get where he was by sitting back and waiting for the world to give him what he needed. He was many things, but complacent was not one of them.

As far as I could tell, none of the guys on the team were. I had yet to meet a lot of them, but if they were anything like him and Frost, I couldn't wait.

He grinned. "No you won't, but that'll be half the fun. When I'm ready, I'll show you the rest of myself. I'll use you the way I want to, like you deserve to be used. We'll need a safe word."

"Yes, we will," I agreed. "Something easy to say, but that can't be mistaken for anything else. Something like...unicorn."

He grimaced. "Unicorn will remind me of Jay. I don't want to be thinking of him while I'm fucking you." When I gave him a funny look, he added, "Jay has some weird fetish about unicorns. I don't think he got hugged enough as a kid." He didn't look like he sympathised very much.

Jayden Lang was one of the players I had yet to meet. From what I could see, there wasn't much love lost between him and Storm.

"Not unicorn then," I said. "What about thunder?"

"As in thunderstorm?" Storm looked amused. "That sounds like something you should be shouting when I'm buried inside you. What about watermelon? Not too many other words sound like that, and it's probably not going to slip out of your lips when you come. Probably."

He rested a hand lightly on my stomach, fingers moving up and down the smooth, flat expanse of my skin. The gesture was more intimate than I would have suspected he was capable of. He was a complicated man. Sometimes gentle, sometimes harder than a rock. He could break me into a thousand pieces, but then he could also put me back together.

I smiled and shrugged. "Works for me." I couldn't wait to see if he'd push me far enough to need a safe word. My limits might be further than he realised. I suspected he'd show me they were further than I realised.

Yes, please.

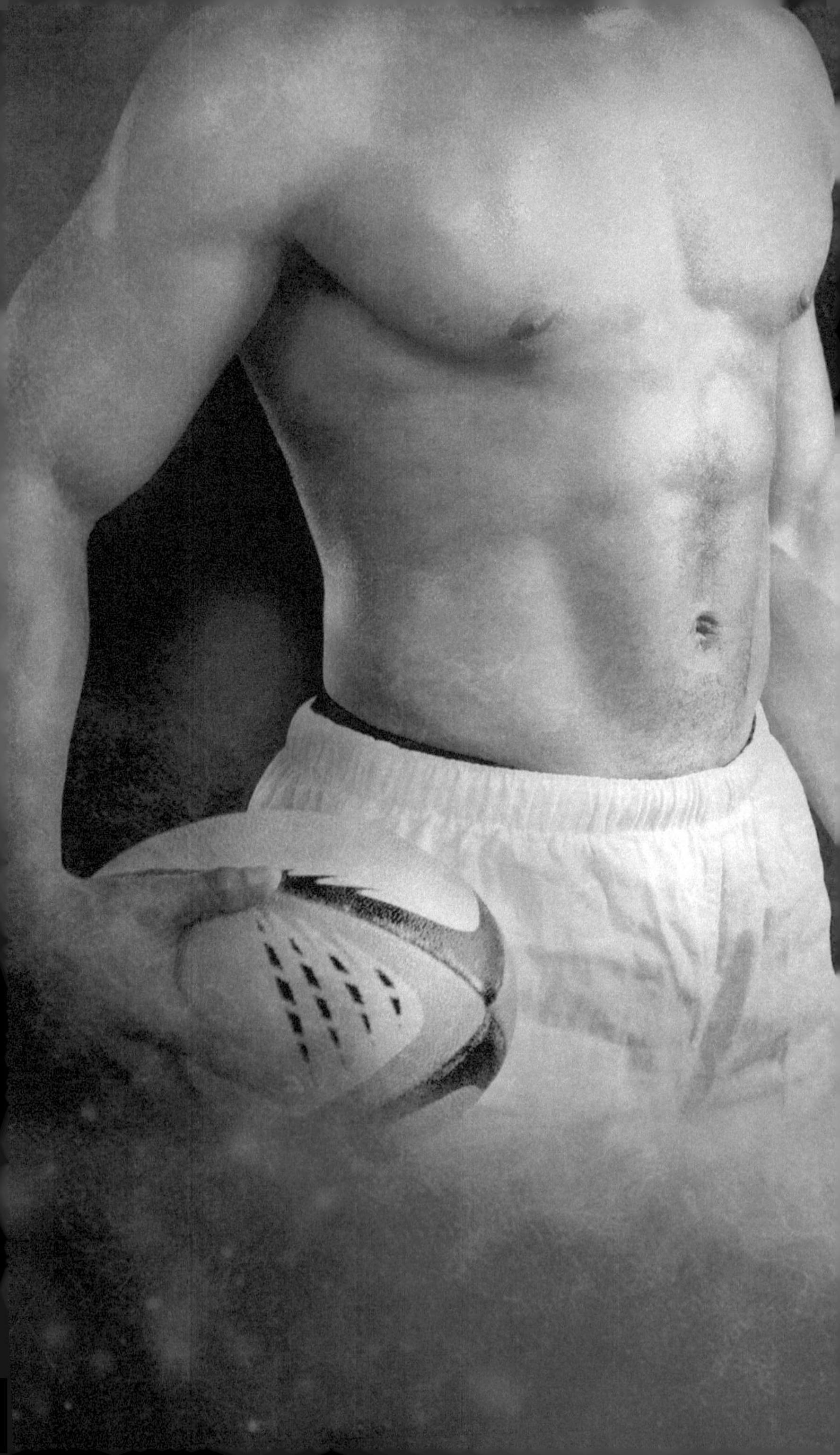

Chapter Fifteen

Storm

I cornered Frost outside the locker room first thing. Before he even saw me, I'd grabbed his arm and shoved him into a small storage room.

"What the fuck?" He glared at me, but he looked about ready to piss his pants. He backed up to the wall as I closed the door and flicked the light on.

"That's my line." I pressed the palm of my hand to the wall beside his head. "She said she took the shit you gave her, on purpose. She said what happened between you and her, she wanted it to happen."

He swallowed visibly. "That's right. She knew exactly what she was doing. Why are you here busting my ass about it?"

I stared at him until he pressed himself harder

against the wall. He looked as though he hoped it would open up and swallow him.

I leaned my upper body back slightly, giving him room to breathe. I wasn't here to intimidate him, not right now. I had other questions that needed answers. "I didn't know this about you. Have you done it before?"

"No," he said quickly. "I wanted to, but most girls wouldn't, you know... But she's not most girls."

I did know. This preference, it wasn't the kind of thing you brought up in casual conversation, even if you were sleeping with a woman.

'Hey, do you mind if I drug you senseless and fuck you?' I had to give him credit for being able to bring it up with Chelsea. I would have liked to be a fly on the wall during that little conversation.

"No she isn't," I agreed. "She knows what she wants, and she likes to try new things."

I'd done a lot of experimentation with a lot of women, but none of them held my attention the way she did.

"Yes, she does," Frost said. "So you're not pissed off at me? I didn't force myself on her." He looked at me sideways, still anxious. Still with a wall behind him and nowhere to run if I decided to punch him. If

I wanted to, I could beat the snot out of him right here and now.

"Not pissed off; I'm curious," I said. "The stuff you gave her, would you take it yourself?"

I got my answer in the way his eyes darkened in response. His breath hitched.

"With the right person," he said finally, carefully.

I leaned in closer, making sure my breath brushed the stubble on his cheeks. "Am I the right person?" I whispered.

He shivered. "I don't know. Maybe."

"Hmmm, maybe isn't a no." I breathed in the scent of him, soap and a touch of arousal.

His lips moved, but no words came out. He looked back at me, blue eyes wide.

He was so close, I could have grazed my mouth over his, slid my tongue between his lips. I could have claimed him the way I claimed Chelsea.

Instead, I stepped back. "We should get to training."

He blinked a couple of times, like he was reminding himself where we were and why we were here. "Training. Right. We don't want to be late for that."

"No, we don't," I said. I turned my back on him and stepped out of the storage room.

I barely made it a metre when Dallas caught up to me.

"What the hell was that?" he insisted.

"Just Frosty and I having a conversation," I said lightly. What did he think? We weren't in the storage room for long enough to get off.

"I meant last night," he said in a harsh whisper. "She was right there and you took her away."

I stopped and turned to look at him. "As opposed to what? Leave her there? She was vulnerable."

"To people like us," he said.

It took me a moment to realise what he was implying. "I didn't take her back to my place and rape her, if that's what you're trying to suggest. I took her to my place and let her sleep it off."

He rubbed a hand over the back of his head. "And that's it? You didn't touch her? What about Frost?" He gestured in the direction the prop had gone, toward the locker room to get ready for training.

"What about him?" I asked. "He had her permission. She told me herself."

"She let him do that to her?" He sounded awed, then shook his head. "I can't stop thinking about her. I can't fucking sleep. All I can think about is her mouth, her body. I could have had her last night."

"Not in the condition she was in," I snapped. "She couldn't have given you her consent."

He looked as though he didn't care either way, he would have taken her.

I was tempted to rearrange his face.

"You don't understand," he said, his voice shaky. "I need her."

"You need to get your asses out there on the paddock," Coach Stanley called out from the doorway.

"Coming, Coach," I said over my shoulder. To Dallas I said, "You need to get a grip. Let's get out there and work off some excess frustration."

I'd seen men obsessed with a woman before, but he looked like an addict in need of a fix. I wasn't sure if I should find a time for him to fuck Chelsea as soon as possible, or if I should keep him as far away from her as I could.

"Come with me to Flirts tonight." I checked the laces on my boots before stepping out onto the field. The autumn weather was perfect for a good, hard training session.

"She'll be there?" he asked eagerly.

"Probably." I started a slow warmup trot around the perimeter of the field. If she wasn't, I'd set him up with someone else so he could burn off some steam.

Maybe he could get obsessed with one of the other dancers.

He grinned. "I'm so there." He nodded and jogged faster, leaving me a few paces behind.

"Is he sure?" Frost asked as he caught up to me. "If I had to guess, I'd say he's not all there."

"You could say that about any of us," I said. "Especially Jay and Atlas."

They must have heard their names, because they turned around to glare at me.

"Fuck off, Keller," Jay snapped.

"Careful, you might hurt his boyfriend's feelings." Atlas sneered at Frost like he was something he might scrape off the bottom of his shoe.

"Careful, your jealousy is showing," I retorted. "You're salty because neither Frost or I would give you the time of day."

"I have better taste than the bottom of the barrel," Atlas said.

I glanced over at Frost and grinned. "At least he can finally admit he wants a boyfriend. The women of Dusk Bay can sleep safe in their beds tonight."

Atlas growled and charged at me, his shoulder dropped before he slammed it into my chest. The momentum carried us both backwards.

I fell on my ass, taking him down to the ground

with me. Rolling over, I slammed my fist into his face.

He aimed his knee at my groin, but caught the side of my thigh instead. My response to that was to punch him again, and again.

Someone grabbed the back of my jersey and pulled me up off him. Frost and Dallas.

Jay and Ramsey grabbed Atlas before he could lunge back at me again.

"Ten more laps to burn off whatever bullshit is going on," Coach snapped. "Any more of that and you're both out."

I spat in the direction of Atlas' boots before heading off at a faster jog.

"He's a fucking prick," I snarled under my breath.

"You need to stop provoking him," Frost said. "Sooner or later he might get a punch in. Wouldn't want him ruining that pretty face of yours."

I snorted. "He couldn't punch his way out of a wet tissue. I don't know what he's doing on the team."

The problem was, neither did he. The Smashers weren't his first choice. Probably not even his second. Ever since he and Jay joined the team, morale was in the toilet.

"You're not helping." Ferris Ramsey caught up to run beside me.

I looked over to him. Three words was more than he usually said in any given sentence. If he could express himself in one, or even none, he would. Sometimes, it was frustrating as hell, but it was a vast improvement on people who talked when they had nothing to say.

"I'm very helpful," I said. "I'm over here supporting my teammates. The ones who aren't dickheads."

His look suggested that was exactly the kind of thing he was referring to. I supposed calling the other guys names was juvenile, but if the hat fit.

"What do you want me to do?" I demanded. "Kiss their asses and call them ice cream? I'm not going to suck up to those two. They wouldn't do the same to me either."

"Bury the hatchet," he said simply. "Not in each other." He gave me a curt nod before jogging faster to catch up with Jay and Atlas.

"In each other sounds good," I said under my breath. "Hey, Frosty, did you bring your hatchet to training?"

He grinned. "Shit, I knew I forgot something. I left it in the pocket of my other shorts."

"I feel sorry for you if your hatchet is so small it fits in your pocket," I teased.

"My hatchet is huge," he said. "So big I can barely pick it up."

"I bet you have no trouble wrapping your hand around it," I said. Now I was picturing him with his cock in his hand, the tip glistening with pre-cum. I tried not to think about licking it off. If anyone was going to lick anything, it would be him licking my cock.

"I usually need two hands," he said. "But you wouldn't know anything about that."

"Don't make me tell you to fuck off," I said jokingly. I'd seen him naked plenty of times before. My cock was more than a match for his. I had nothing to worry about in that department. Neither did he, if I was honest.

"You wouldn't do that to me," he said, smiling that smile of his that made him look a lot more innocent than he actually was.

I couldn't help remembering him lying on top of Chelsea, having just come inside her. The groans as he orgasmed, echoed through my ears. Almost as compelling as hers.

The memory made my cock stir in the front of my pants. Couple that with the way it felt to be buried deep inside her this morning. So fucking good and tight. Such a relief after having soaped her up in the bath and rinsed her off. I'd washed her hair, between her legs, everywhere. At each moment, battling with the desire to join her in the bath and sink into her.

I was no gentleman, but last night I had to pretend. I had to contain myself, to keep from doing something I'd regret. Now I had her consent, I didn't have to hold back next time. But last night, I had no choice. Last night I had to be one of the good guys. Better that than having to grovel later for her forgiveness.

Storm Keller didn't grovel.

I was careful to walk the line so I didn't fuck up in the first place. Sometimes that line was thin as hell.

"I'd think about it," I said. Along with a bunch of other things I'd do to him. It might be time to stop fighting my attraction to Daniel Frost. Stop fighting and admit I wanted to fuck him boneless.

"You know how to hurt a guy," he said.

"Yeah, I do," I replied. "And I know how to make you enjoy every second of it."

He gaped at me for a few long moments before Coach called us over to start on drills.

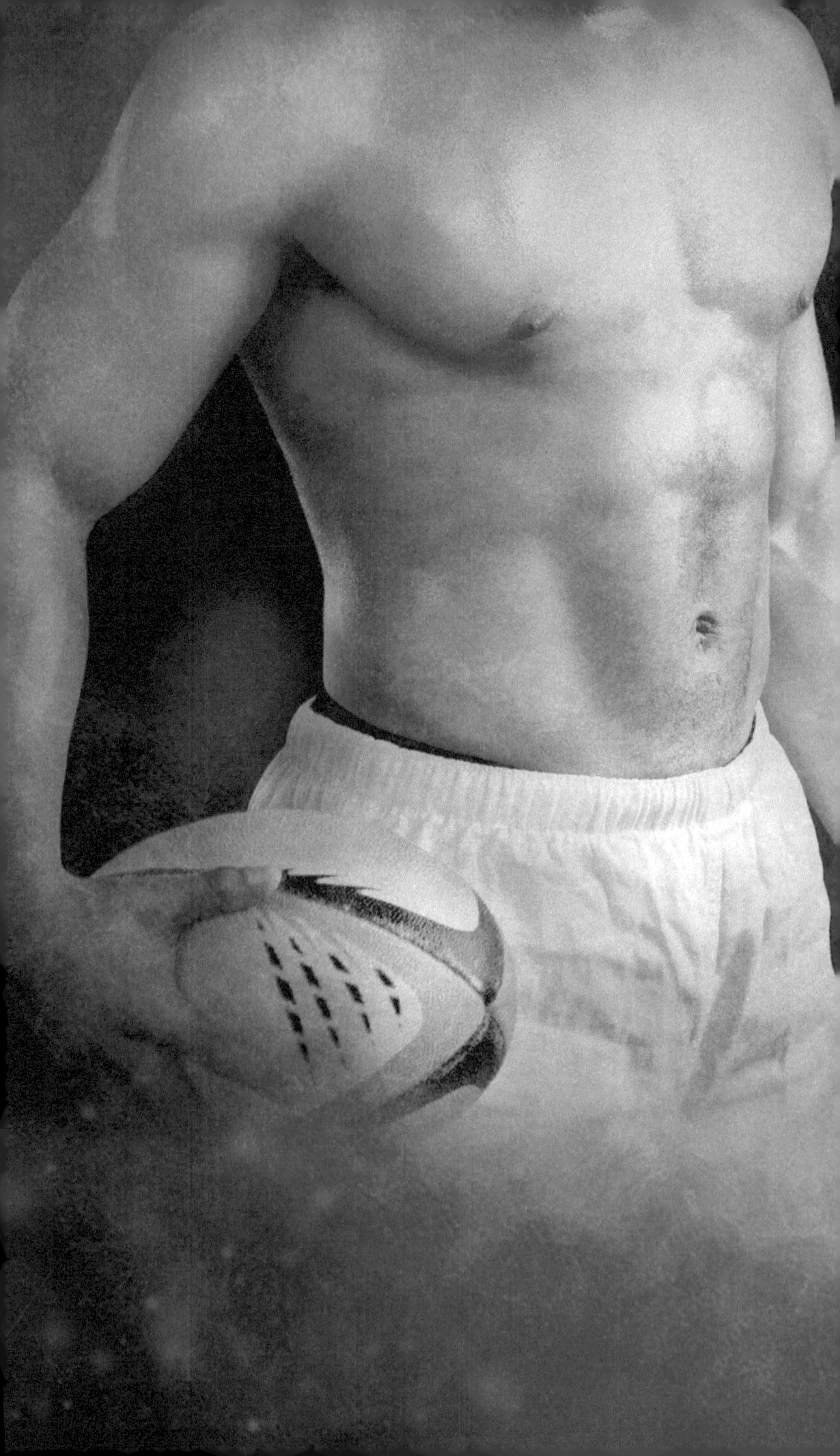

Chapter Sixteen

Chelsea

"We're going to miss you. Are you sure you won't stay for a while longer?" Divina pouted. Her purple hair was held back in a messy bun. Her eyebrow piercing glinted in the light from the phone permanently glued to her hand.

"I'm sure," I said. "Tonight will be my last night." I'd miss dancing at Flirts, but I wanted to concentrate on medicine now. The hours I was putting into both had become exhausting and, thanks to Storm, I'd be all right for money for a while.

"You know you can come back any time." She gave me a hug. "I'll always make room for you on the roster. The customers are going to miss you *almost* as much as I will."

"They probably won't even notice." I hugged her back.

"Of course they will," she insisted. "The other girls are amazing, but they aren't you."

I caught a hint of movement behind her and looked over her shoulder to see Ivy glare at me.

For some reason, the stunning blonde had taken a dislike to me. I had no idea why. She was talented, beautiful and captivating. I'd never done anything to her, and she had no reason to be jealous of me that I was aware of.

I smiled at her anyway, but she curled her lip and turned away. Whatever her problem was, it was hers. I wasn't going to make it mine.

"Get up on that stage and shake your booty one last time," Divina said. "If you're really going to leave us, then you better make it count."

"When do I not?" I smiled.

I sat down to push my feet into my stilettos and stepped out onto the stage. I wasn't surprised to see Storm, Frost and Dallas at the front of the stage.

Storm looked like he was proud of me, as though he might in some way take credit for my performance.

Frost was smiling, more relaxed than I'd seen him before.

Ivy walked past him and gave him a long glance, but he didn't seem to notice.

I remembered that they'd spent time in one of the private rooms together. Ivy might have been hoping for a second round.

He seemed oblivious to the fact she still existed. Was that what had her pissed off at me? No, she'd always been terse with me. Whatever. I probably wouldn't see her again after tonight.

Dallas stood beside Frost, his hands at his sides, framing the bulge that strained the front of his pants. His eyes were glued to me like I was the only person sharing the planet with him. The club could have erupted in a riot and he wouldn't have noticed. Every drop of his attention was on me.

The music started and I began my routine, dividing my attention between the three players. Would they be disappointed I wasn't going to be dancing here after tonight? They seemed to enjoy coming to watch.

Maybe I'd give them a private show someday, if they were lucky.

I peeled off my clothes, careful to make sure my underwear stayed away from Storm. I shot him a smile to let him know I remembered he'd taken my panties the last time.

He grinned unashamedly. Of course he would. That was who he was. Nothing kept him down for long.

I kept waiting for him to make a move, like we'd talked about. Grab me when I was getting out of my car and 'abduct' me, or something. So far he hadn't. What was he waiting for? The right time, or for me to lower my guard? Maybe both.

I spun around a couple more times before giving the crowd a curtsy and hurrying backstage.

"Another exciting performance," Ivy said caustically. She treated me to a slow clap.

"I thought so," I said lightly. I walked over to my small cupboard and pulled out fresh clothes. "I'm sure you'll enjoy the extra limelight when I'm gone."

"I deserve it," she said. "I should have had your spot a long time ago."

"If you say so." I shrugged and pulled a T-shirt over my head.

"I do say so." She stalked over to me. "You think you're so perfect."

"Do I?" I pulled the T-shirt into place. "I wouldn't have thought so, but you seem to know more about me than I do." She was beginning to piss me off.

"I know you're a conceited bitch," she snapped.

"You think you're so much better than the rest of us. You don't even need to be here."

"What do you know about what I need?" I snapped back.

She placed her hands on her curvy hips. "Don't pretend you don't know. Your family has plenty of money. You don't need it. You being here took money from people who did."

"People like you?" I guessed.

"Exactly," she said resentfully. "Who does something like that?"

"Someone who doesn't want to rely on her family's money," I replied. "Someone who wants to stand on her own two feet, even if that means dancing in stilettos. Or getting naked and fucking strangers. I did it for the same reason you did, for the money. And for the enjoyment. Because I loved working here."

I cocked my head at her. "You're starting to make me think I shouldn't leave. I love taking my clothes off for admiring strangers. Don't you?"

She glared at me like she wanted to wipe the smile off my face. "Flirts doesn't need you to stay."

"Because the club has you," I said with thinly veiled sarcasm. "How lucky for them. Divina must adore the ground you walk on, because you bring so much joy."

"She will when you're gone and she can finally see me past you," Ivy said. "Those guys too." She waved towards the stage. "They'll forget you the moment you're gone. If they even know what you look like. You were nothing more than something for their cock to do. Now they'll have my pussy."

"If I was you, I'd get a better therapist. The one you're seeing doesn't seem to be helping." I smoothed down my hair and stepped towards the doorway.

"And if I was you, I'd watch my fucking back," she said. "Just in case."

I turned back around, but she just smiled.

I smiled back, but my expression wasn't pleasant. "You must be dumber than you look if you're really threatening me. You have no idea what I'm capable of. Do you know who my family is?"

For the first time, she looked uncertain. She tried to cover it with bravado. "Nothing I can't handle. It's not like I haven't...handled your father."

I snorted. "As if my father would fuck you." Either my mother or my brother would have him slowly eviscerated if he did. If he didn't eviscerate himself. He loved my mother too much to cheat, especially with someone like Ivy.

"Think whatever you want to think," she said. "I know what the truth is."

"Is there a problem?" Storm peered through the doorway leading into the changing area. He barely glanced in Ivy's direction. "You coming, Chels? We're waiting for you. Dallas is about to come in his pants."

"We wouldn't want that," I said. I gave Ivy a half glance before walking past her and out the door.

"It must be the day for it," Storm muttered.

"Trouble at work?" I asked.

He put an arm around me. "Nothing I can't handle."

We stepped out to the quieter part of the club, where Frost and Dallas were waiting.

"Hey." Frost gave me a kiss on the cheek. "I understand you've met Dallas."

Dallas hadn't taken his eyes off me since I approached, and he didn't now. He looked like he was ready to jump out of his skin. His cock was ready to jump out of the front of his pants.

"We met," I said. I gave Dallas a kiss on the cheek. His face promptly turned red.

"It seems like Dallas is a big fan of yours," Storm said.

"I... I..." Dallas stammered.

"Forgive him, he's currently unable to think with anything but his cock," Frost said. "Storm thinks you should put him out of his misery."

"My treat," Storm said.

I placed my hand on Dallas' hard bicep, and leaned in to say, "If that's what you really want? You seemed upset the other night." I wasn't going to pressure him into doing anything he didn't want to do. He got caught up in the moment once, he could get caught up again, and add to his regrets. As far as I was concerned, life was too short for those. Live in the moment and don't look back, that was my motto. Take life by the balls and ride it hard.

"I freaked out," he said in a rush. "I want you. I want you so fucking much." He placed his hands on my hips and drew me to him so I could feel his cock pressing against me. "Right now."

"Here?" I replied. "In front of everyone in the club?"

Many of the customers preferred privacy, but others didn't. Some nights, you couldn't turn around without tripping over another couple fucking. Or several, all screwing each other. As long as everyone was enjoying themselves and each other, Divina didn't care. We were making her money, that was what mattered. That and keeping the customers satisfied.

Dallas groaned in my ear.

I took that as a positive. I reached between us and ran the heel of my hand up and down his erection. He was iron hard already. Thick and throbbing.

He hurried to undo his pants until his cock sprang free. He grabbed my hand and wrapped my fingers around his length. Eyes half-closed, he thrust into my hand a couple of times before tugging at the hem of my skirt.

"I don't want to come in your hand," he said. He scrunched up his face with the effort to keep from coming too soon.

I pulled a condom out of my pocket and opened it before rolling it onto him. I still worked here for another couple of hours, so I'd obey Divina's rules.

Holding him carefully, I stepped back to an empty couch to the side of the room. I lay down, taking him with me, until he was lying on top of me.

"I need to be inside you," he said urgently.

"Yes please," I told him. "I want to feel you." His desperate need was contagious. If I didn't have his cock buried in my pussy in the next couple of minutes, I might go out of my mind.

He pushed my skirt and panties aside and parted

my legs with his knees. With one push, he buried himself all the way inside me. He moaned softly, his lips apart, eyes crossed. "You feel fucking incredible."

"She does, doesn't she?" Storm said.

"She really does," Frost agreed. "Dallas is a lucky prick right now."

"For now," Storm agreed. "Later, it will be our turn."

They sat down on chairs in front of us to watch as Dallas fucked me frantically, any ounce of control completely gone. He was like an animal, pounding over and over, driving us both hard to the edge. The second-rower held back absolutely nothing, just like he did on the field. Everything he had, he gave to me.

I gladly took it, loving the way his thick cock felt in my wet heat. Wanting more, more, more.

I came first, arching my back and crying out, turned on by his relentless fucking and the eyes on us. My muscles contracted around him, drawing out his own orgasm.

He tipped back his head and shouted triumphantly as he spilled himself into the condom inside me. "Fucking hell. You're fucking everything."

He slumped down, puffing lightly. He shook his head. "I'm so sorry. I didn't want to be so..." He tried to compose his words, but nothing else would come. Nothing but regret, but this time it wasn't because of who I was. That didn't seem to matter to him anymore.

"It's okay," I assured him. "Sometimes all you need is a quick, hard fuck. But now, we can have a long, slow one." I wrapped my legs around him, hooked my feet together and started to roll my hips, making him hard all over again.

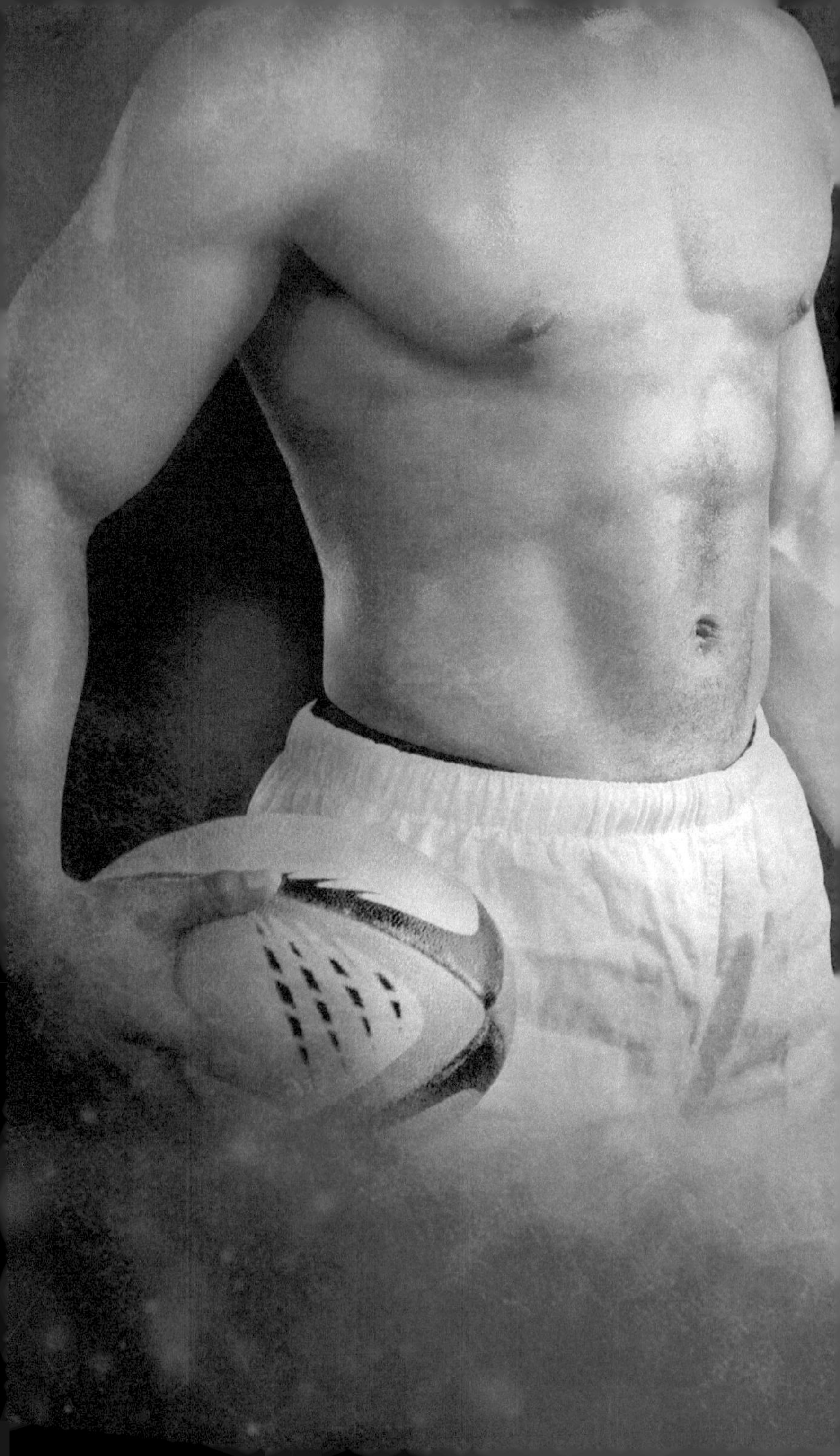

Chapter Seventeen

Chelsea

"I must say you've lightened the work load significantly," Doctor Stuart said. "These physicals would have taken much longer without you. Just our bad luck losing two of our staff right before the season started." He rubbed at his temples.

"I'm happy to be here," I said cheerfully. "Whatever you throw at me, I'll be happy to catch it."

He sighed. "If it wasn't against the rules, I'd insist they hire you now. You've been a breath of fresh air around here, and continuing placement seems like a monumental waste of time."

"If it wasn't against the rules, I'd let them hire me," I said with a grin. I tempered my enthusiasm a little and asked, "What do you think my chances are of being able to work here when my placement is finished?"

"If it was up to me, two hundred percent," he said. "All I can do is put in my recommendation and hope management agrees. I don't want to toot my horn too loudly, but my recommendation holds some weight. It should, after all these years."

He handed me a clipboard and gestured to the treatment room. "If you can do the last three, that would be perfect. I'll be downstairs observing a couple of injured players and assessing their recovery. No doubt they'll be eager to get a clean bill of health."

"I'm sure they will," I replied. I could just imagine how restless they'd get, having to take things easy for a while. Personally, I'd be climbing the walls.

He nodded as he slipped out of the room, leaving me to look down at the clipboard.

I grimaced to myself.

"Hey..." Dallas froze in the doorway.

"Hey, yourself," I said as though I hadn't just surprised the hell out of him. "Come on in."

"What are you doing here?" He didn't move. His eyes were wide, and his pants immediately tented. He blinked a couple of times, as if trying to see if I was real.

"I'm here to give you your physical," I said. "To assess your fitness to play this season."

Before he thought I meant the other kind of physical.

He shook his head. "I don't get it. You're a..." He pressed his lips together.

"Whore?" I suggested with venomous sweetness. I thought we got past that the previous night, but evidently we hadn't.

"Yes," he said without thinking. "I mean—" He gaped like his jaw had springs. "I didn't mean... I meant..." He ran a hand over the back of his head.

"I know what you meant," I said coldly. "Storm paid me to fuck you and I did. But I'm here as a medical professional. Don't worry, I'm fully qualified. I'm guessing he and Frost didn't tell you who I was."

"They knew?" That seemed to hit him like a punch to the face.

"Yes, they knew," I said.

"Why didn't you say something?" His face turned pink, eyes now flashing with annoyance, bordering on barely contained rage. "Did you think I wouldn't find out?"

"I don't owe you any explanation," I said, trying to keep my voice even. "What I do at Flirts and what

I do here are separate. Just like if you played football during the day and flipped burgers at night. That would be no one's business."

He stepped towards me, hands curled into fists so tight his knuckles were white. "It's my business if the whore who was paid to fuck me turns up at my place of work."

He took a moment to let his own words sink in, and the colour drained from his face.

"Is that what this is about? What do you really want? If the team finds out, I'm done." He looked like he might wrap his hands around my throat and strangle me to keep me from saying a word.

"Unless you're planning to tell them, they won't know. Like I said, my two jobs are separate. At least, they were. I put in my resignation last night. I'm hoping the team will hire me full-time in a couple of weeks. Are you going to have a problem with that?"

He could decide to make things difficult for me. He seemed volatile at the best of times. Did he regret what we did last night, after all? At the time, he seemed to enjoy himself.

He slumped against the wall, leaning his weight on his shoulder, and shook his head, his mouth open. "Nothing about this makes sense. You're not supposed to be here."

"I'm not?" I picked up the lanyard that lay around my neck and held out the identification card. "This says otherwise."

He was starting to make me nervous. He could run out the door, straight to management, and get me booted out. Of course, they'd want to know how he knew what I did, but he could make up anything. He was one of the team's star players, whatever he told them, they'd listen.

"Why here?" he asked. "Why me? What do you really want?"

"I just want to do my job," I said, trying to contain my frustration. "My *medical* job. As for why you, it's just my job."

His head jerked back like I'd hit him. "Just your job," he whispered. "Fucking me was just your job."

I decided not to address that out loud. There was more to last night than that. I'd *enjoyed* screwing him.

I reminded myself if it wasn't him, it would have been someone else.

"Why did Storm pay you to be with me?" His brow creased deeply, showing grooves across his forehead.

"You'd have to ask him that," I said. "I guess he was being nice." And he was trying to choose who I fucked. Not to mention he seemed to enjoy watching. For him, it was all about control. It turned him on to have control over me. It turned me on to let him.

"He knew how much I wanted you," Dallas whispered. "You're all I can think about. I haven't been sleeping, I can hardly eat."

"Is this where you say that wouldn't have been the case if you knew I'd turn up here?" I asked. "Because everything that happened at Flirts was only supposed to be a fantasy?"

In the minds of some men, women like me weren't supposed to exist in the real world. We were there for them to get off, then we disappeared into the backs of their minds. We weren't of the same world as their wives, girlfriends, or daughters.

Except that we were.

He closed his eyes tight. "Women like you don't give a shit about guys like me."

"Who hurt you?" I asked without thinking. Was that too blunt? Possibly, but the words were out and I couldn't take them back.

"Ex-girlfriend," he said without opening his eyes. "She cheated. Walked in on them together."

"And since then, you're sure of...what? That women just want to use you?"

He opened his eyes and shrugged one shoulder. "Most of them only give a shit because I play for the Smashers. They only want what they can get from me, then they fuck off. You're not any different."

I grimaced. "Ouch. Believe it or not, I don't want anything from you. I don't need you in order to raise my social media profile. I don't need your money. At least, I won't when I get my job here. I don't even need you to like me. What I do need is for you to step into the treatment room so we can start your physical."

"Did you hate it?" he asked.

"Hate what?" I pushed a few stray strands of hair off my face and tried to contain my irritation at his stubbornness. Doctor Stuart wasn't going to be impressed if he got back and I wasn't finished. Not to mention that another player would be along soon.

If there was anything in the world I didn't like, it was wasting time.

"Fucking me," he insisted. "You only did it because you got paid. Otherwise you wouldn't have. Why would you fuck anyone for money?"

"Because I don't hate it," I said as evenly as I could. "I like sex, and I like eating."

He looked confused.

"In order to eat, I need money," I said. "I guess

you could say I like sex and I like money. And I liked having sex with you. I've never faked my enjoyment, and I never will."

"You really came around my cock?" He still looked disbelieving.

"All three of those orgasms were real," I said. "And very much appreciated, thank you."

"What about Storm and Frost?" He glanced toward the door, as if he suddenly remembered where we were.

"They gave me orgasms too," I said. "Well, Storm did, the other morning, but Frost got me started the night before. So that counts. If you're wondering if I liked being with them too, I did. Believe it or not, I can have sex without being paid."

The bulge in his pants visibly increased, straining the seams. "You're really not working there any more?"

"Unless working here falls through, then no," I said. "I'm not working there anymore."

"No more taking your clothes off for strangers?" he asked.

I cocked my head and smiled. "I wouldn't rule that out, but not in that environment. Not in this one either, before you make any suggestions. I don't think the team would look very favourably upon me for stripping in here when I'm supposed to be doing physicals."

"There's no one here but us," he pointed out. He pushed himself off the wall and stepped towards me. "No one would know."

"We have a limited amount of time for your physical," I said. "Someone will walk in sooner or later. One of your teammates, or maybe one of the coaches."

"Then we better hurry." He took my hand and pulled me into the treatment room. With a firm click, he closed the door behind us.

"We can't do this here," I protested, but an edge of excitement started to creep through me.

"Yes, we can." He grabbed my wrists in one hand and pinned them to the wall above my head. "You're not being paid for this. Prove to me you wanted me."

"Dallas—" I started.

"Shhh, prove you weren't lying. Prove you weren't faking it." He tugged down the front of my blouse and the cup of my bra and leaned down to fasten his lips around my nipple.

"We really shouldn't," I protested one more time. But then my hands were working the front of his pants, pulling them down so I could wrap my hands around his cock.

"Yes, we should," he whispered. "I need you, Chelsea. I'm going to fuck you and I'm going to come inside you."

He let go of my wrists, turned me around and bent me over the treatment table. He pushed up my skirt, and pushed down my panties. They slipped down my legs and onto the floor before I kicked them off.

I barely had time to take another breath before he was parting my legs and notching his cock at my entrance.

"I couldn't stop myself if I wanted to," he said with a groan. He pushed all the way into me, his bare cock sliding to the hilt. "You make me lose control. All I want to do is be inside you. Fucking you is all I can think about." He sounded like an addict, desperate to fulfil his need.

He pounded into me quickly, frantically, like the first time we fucked the night before. Like if he didn't thrust as hard as he could, he might lose his mind.

I reached down to rub my clit while he rammed into me, grunting like a wild animal.

"I'm going to come," he panted. "I'm going to come inside you."

"Yes," I breathed. "Yes please." I rubbed harder, close as well. "Come with me."

He moaned and came at the same time I did, muscles contracting, bodies slick against each other.

I felt the warmth of his cum spill inside me as I was enveloped in a universe of bliss.

"Fuck, yeah," he groaned. "Your pussy is fucking everything. Fucking mine."

We both sagged over the table, puffing and panting.

"We really should do this physical," I said when I finally caught my breath.

"I think we just did," he said.

I snorted a laugh. "Okay, but let's do the proper kind now."

Reluctantly, he slid out of me and pulled his pants back up. "If you're going to work here, you're going to need to get used to this. Whenever I need a fuck, I'm going to come to you and take one. You'll have your own office then. We can go in there."

"If I have the time," I said.

He fixed me with a firm look. "You'll make time." He sat on the treatment table like I didn't have his cum trickling down my thighs, and offered me his arm to check his blood pressure.

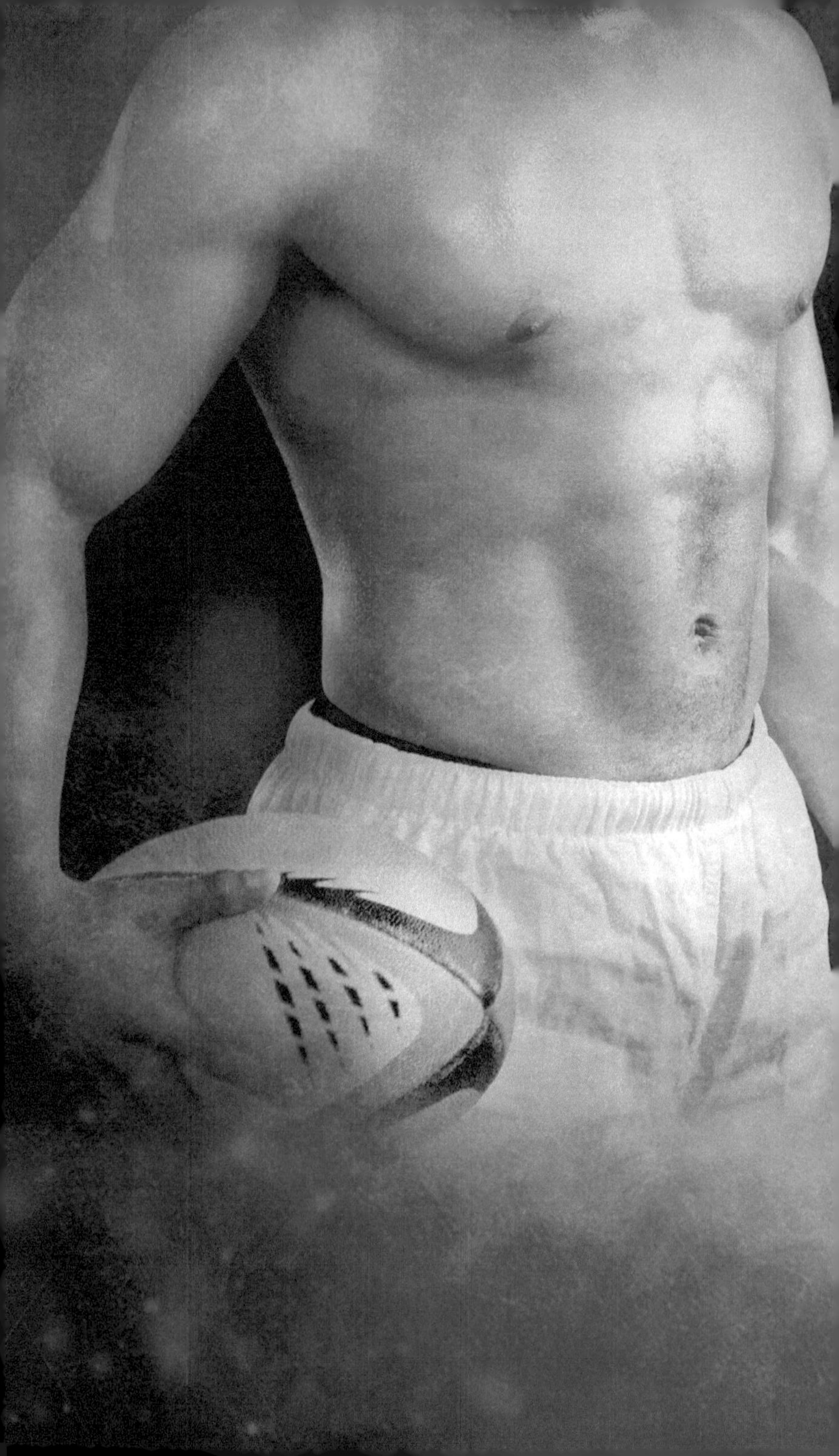

Chapter Eighteen

Chelsea

Dallas was waiting for me when I finished at the end of the day. He stood near the doorway, watching while I finished checking over one of his teammates.

"Thank you, you're free to go now," I said cheerfully. "I don't think there will be any problem with you playing on the weekend."

"Thanks, Doc." The breakaway smiled. He was one of the youngest members of the team, and one of the most recent recruits. This would be his first season playing, and he was eager to prove himself.

"You're welcome." I gave him a nod before he hurried away.

Dallas watched him leave, his lips pressed tight together. "Have dinner with me."

"Dinner?" I echoed.

I stepped over to drop the clipboard onto Doctor Stuart's desk. Once I was done with Dallas, the rest of the day went smoothly. The other guys on the team did their physicals without any protest. If they cared about having a female doctor, none of them gave any sign. It was refreshing. I hoped the other handful would be as easy.

"You said you like to eat," he insisted. "Have dinner with me. We can eat and maybe then I can convince you to take your clothes off. I'd be more than happy to take mine off for you." He dropped his hands to the waistband of his pants and teased that he might push them down his thighs.

"She has plans." Storm stepped into the infirmary.

"Yeah, with me," Frost followed him in.

"As it happens, I don't have any plans," I told all of them.

Nothing concrete, although I figured one of them would show up sooner or later. I hadn't expected all three of them. What would happen if things got serious between me and one of these guys? Things could get ugly between them.

"Yes, you do," Storm said. "You can have dinner with all of us."

Dallas and Frost both frowned at him.

"All of us?" Frost echoed. "What the fuck are you talking about?"

"I'm talking about the fact we're all into this woman." Storm nodded towards me. "I've already laid claim to her, and so has Frost."

"So have I," Dallas said quickly.

"Do I have any say in this?" I asked dryly.

Three pairs of eyes turned towards me, all with the same expression in them.

I raised my hands to either side. "That was what I thought."

None of them was giving me a choice. They'd chosen me. All three of them were determined I was theirs. I was a confident woman, but I never would have expected to find myself in this situation. With three possessive, insanely hot rugby players laying claim to me.

"Good girl," Storm said. He turned back to the others. "She belongs to all of us. Unless one of you is going to back off, then we can all eat dinner together tonight."

"I'm not backing off," Frost said. "Dinner works for me." His eyes were dark, his gaze shifting back and forth between me and Storm. It wasn't just me he wasn't backing away from. His attraction to the big fullback was becoming more and more obvious. To me, if not to them.

"Dinner is cool," Dallas said. "I made a booking. I'll update it."

Of course he made a booking for us before asking. Was he even really asking? What would he have done if I said no?

He was right though, I did say I liked food, and frankly I was too hungry to argue anyway. If three guys wanted to take me out, then who was I to stop them?

"Do it," Storm told him.

Dallas gave him the side eye, but pulled out his phone and got to work updating the booking.

"Just out of curiosity..." Frost started.

"Bring it, but don't use it until I say so," Storm replied.

It took me a moment to realise he was talking about whatever drug Frost slipped me.

A flutter of excitement travelled through me. The idea of all three of them taking me while I was helpless to fight them off was compelling as hell. On the other hand, I also liked to be an active participant in sex.

I'd wait and see what the night held.

"Consider it brought," Frost said. He patted the pocket of his track pants.

"Did I mention how fucked up that was?" Dallas asked.

"Yeah, but on a scale of one to ten, how much do you like fucked up?" Frost asked him.

I picked up my bag and phone and laughed at the expression on Dallas' face. "He's got you there. I think we all might be a bit more fucked up than normal."

"I know I am," Storm said. "But I'd wear it on a T-shirt." He held up his hands to make air quotes. "'Fucked up as fuck.'"

"The club would love it if the paparazzi took photos of you with a shirt like that on it," Frost said sarcastically. "Can you hear that?" He put a hand to his ear. "That's the sound of them tearing up his contract."

"They'd tear up yours if they knew you were at Flirts," Storm said dryly.

"They'd tear all of ours up," Dallas said. His relaxed expression was replaced with worry.

"Then let's hope they don't find out," Frost said. "Personally, I have no need to go there again. Not if Chelsea isn't working there anymore."

"Me either." Storm patted Dallas on the back of his shoulder. "Chill out, bro. Can we enjoy a night out?"

"Yeah," Dallas said, not looking convinced. "I guess so."

"And I know so," Storm said. "My car is the biggest, I'll drive." He glanced around as though expecting one of them to suggest he was overcompensating. He nodded in satisfaction when neither of them did.

I rolled my eyes at him. Men and their cocks. Lucky for all of us I enjoyed them so much. Otherwise, I might take myself out to dinner. I made a note to do that anyway. Or maybe get Sadie to come out with me. Now I'd have more time, there was no excuse not to spend more of it with her. Sisters before misters, and all that.

I wasn't the kind of girl who'd turn her back on her best friend just because I got the attention of a man, not even men like these. Sadie deserved better than that.

When I told her about them, she was going to lose her mind. Hopefully not like Ivy had but I doubted it. Sadie was too nice to be anything but supportive.

"I'll sit in the back with Chelsea," Frost said. He

favoured me with one of his best smiles. Dimples and all.

Dallas pressed his lips together, and for a moment I thought he might object. "Fine," he said finally. "This time."

I walked in the middle of them as we stepped out of the infirmary, towards the car park. Surrounded by all that muscle, I couldn't help but feel a little bit spoiled. If Ivy could see me now, she'd be ready to spit rocks.

We headed through the darkened car park, over to Storm's SUV. He pressed on the fob to unlock it and we climbed in.

Frost looked back over his shoulder as he closed the door and clicked his seatbelt.

"What is it?" I peered through the rear window, trying to figure out what caught his eye.

He shook his head. "I just had a feeling we were being watched."

"You don't seem to mind being watched," I said, half-teasing, half-concerned he might be right.

Dusk Bay was a dangerous place at times. There was always a possibility I'd become a target because of my family. I tried to stay out of the shit they were involved in, but that wouldn't deter everyone.

"That depends on the circumstances." He

frowned and looked around again. "We should get out of here."

Storm started the engine and drove the car out of the parking space. "You're starting to freak Dallas out."

"Fuck off," Dallas said. "I'm not freaked out." He was also looking out of the car, back in the direction we'd come.

"If that's you not freaked out, I'd hate to see you when you are freaked out," Storm told him. "Do me a favour and stick your dick out the window if you're going to piss yourself."

"I'm not going to—" Dallas turned around to glare at him. "I'm starting to see Jay and Atlas's point."

"They have a point?" Storm asked. He seemed amused, rather than irritated. He'd take Dallas' bait, but he was humouring him.

Dallas glanced over at him, obviously knowing what the other player was doing. "About you being an asshole, they do."

"I never claimed I wasn't an asshole," Storm said easily. "That might be the only thing they have a point about. The rest of the time, they're too busy with their heads up their asses."

"Jayden Lang and Atlas Underwood?" I asked.

They were both incredible players. Of course they had to be, to help take their previous team all the way to the premiership. And now they were here, playing for the Smashers. That had to be a culture shock, to say the least. How did they feel about playing for Dusk Bay? If they were making waves with other players, they might not view the situation favourably. That could mean doing my job would be even more difficult.

I suppressed a groan. I'd cross that bridge when I got to it. For all I knew, they could be cooperative.

A girl could hope. Right?

"That's them," Frost said. "They hate us for some reason. I don't know why, because we're pretty fucking awesome. Ferris Ramsey seems to have taken their side, which makes him as bad as them."

He seemed to see the situation in black and white. Either they were friends, or they were enemies.

I knew better than to think anything in life was that simple. Friends could become enemies and vice versa. Especially in this city. Even ties like family could be severed if someone looked at another person the wrong way. All the more reason to keep my head down and try not to piss too many people off.

"They're all pricks and I have better things to do than think about them," Storm said. "Like the fact that—and I'm no expert here—but it seems like we're being followed."

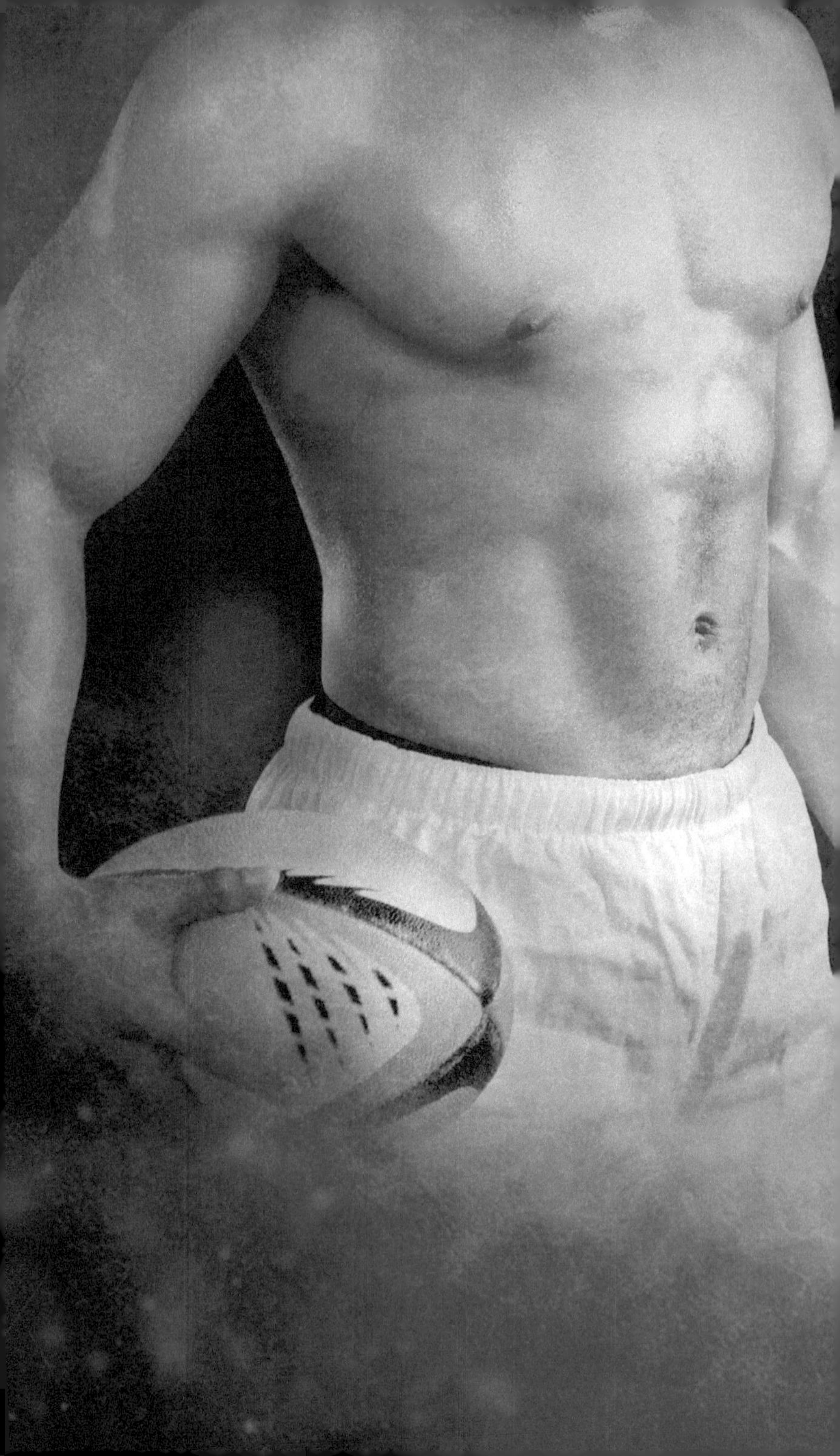

Chapter Nineteen

Storm

My words were met with silence, but it wasn't a shocked one.

"Can you tell who it is?" Frost sat so far forward in his seat, he was practically breathing down the back of my neck.

I squinted at the rear view mirror. "Not really," I said. "Some kind of small car, a red one. Not very subtle." They cruised right behind us, matching our speed, headlights bobbing with each dip on the road.

"They could be going the same way we are," Frost suggested.

Let's test that theory.

I slowed and took the corner a bit too fast. Then the next one straight after.

The red hatchback was still on our bumper.

"We've gone around in a circle and they're still there," I said. "I'm going to pull into the restaurant car park. We'll see what they do." If they were trying to cause problems, we'd deal with them. They might be overzealous fans who saw us and decided they needed selfies with us. Fans got weird sometimes.

"I think we should find somewhere quieter. Where no one else is around," Chelsea said. "We don't know what they want." She sounded nervous, but not scared.

I glanced at her reflection in the rear vision mirror. She was so fucking gorgeous it was a miracle I didn't crash into the car in front of me when they stopped at the red traffic light.

"We can guess." I tapped on the brakes and brought the SUV to an abrupt stop.

Dallas grabbed onto the Jesus handle as the momentum threw him forward.

I ignored his grunt of annoyance and swivelled around in my seat to take a better look behind us.

The hatchback's headlights were too bright for me to make out anything more than a figure seated behind the steering wheel.

"Are you sure?" Chelsea was the only one *not* looking back over her shoulder.

I took in the expression on her face. "What is it?"

"It *might* be nothing," she said. She started to shrug, but dropped her shoulders and closed her mouth over unsaid words.

"You don't think it's nothing," I said.

What the hell did she think it was then? Someone sent to assassinate us? Or kidnap us and use us to create a race of superhumans? That sort of stuff only existed in books and movies. As far as I knew anyway.

"Don't tell us, you're really a spy," Frost said. "Come to Dusk Bay to uncover some nefarious plot to take over the world."

She snorted. "Hardly. But if I was, I wouldn't be able to tell you."

"Not unless you recruited us to help you," he said. "I'd be down for that."

"She's not a spy," I told him. I turned back around in my seat and drove through the green light.

A couple of minutes later, we pulled into the car park. I backed the SUV into an empty space and killed the engine.

The red car parked a few spots away, front end in first, and the driver climbed out. Long legs, blonde hair, camera in her hand, aimed at us.

What a fucking shock.

"Paparazzi," Dallas sneered.

We were professional footballers. The public eye was something we were used to, especially when the season was about to start. The media would like nothing more than to dig up something salacious about us. And if they couldn't find it, they'd make it up.

Only last week, I was reading about the stunning revelation that I was an alien with three cocks and a couple of love children. Whoever wrote that, they had a future in fiction. That sort of shit made me laugh.

Being followed, not so much.

"Don't make eye contact," I said. "Don't engage."

"What a pleasant surprise," the leech in human form said, her tone as sleek as her pencil skirt and blouse. "Storm Keller, Daniel Frost and Dallas Gregory. And...friend." She peered at Chelsea.

"Get lost," Dallas growled. He could get away with being unfriendly, but if he told her to fuck off, he could get in trouble with the team. Apparently swearing was a step too far.

I applauded his restraint. I was barely hanging on to my own.

"So much for not engaging," Frost said under his breath. "I recognise her. Belinda Simmons. She works for one of those trashy magazines."

"One person's trash is another person's informative entertainment," Belinda said. "The public deserves to know what people like you get up to off the field. How about you pose for a couple of photos and I'll leave you alone?" She seemed more interested in Chelsea than the rest of us.

My blood went cold. Did she have a clue Chelsea used to work at Flirts? Something like that would make headlines in about ten seconds. I squinted at her. My gut feeling was she didn't know. She spotted us and decided to go digging.

"How about you go away?" Dallas said. "Let's go inside." He stayed close to Chelsea, without touching her. Thank fuck he had that much sense. One photo of them together would raise eyebrows and suspicions.

I was already second-guessing coming here at all. I wanted to put Chelsea in lots of different positions, but this wasn't one of them.

Belinda laughed. "Don't be like that. This doesn't have to be difficult. You smile, I take photos. Those photos go online for all your fans to enjoy. It's really that simple."

"It's an invasion of privacy," Dallas said. "I don't give you permission to take my photo." He stomped over to the restaurant door, opened it and gestured for us to step inside.

"Sweetie, you're in a public place," Belinda said, all condescension and vinegar-laced honey. "How can I invade your privacy when you're not in private?"

"Probably by climbing on a ladder and peering over a fence," Frost told her.

She pretended to look shocked. "I would never do something so tacky."

I couldn't keep quiet any longer. "You followed us. Some people would call that tacky. Some might even suggest it's illegal."

She laughed. "I happened to be driving on the same road as you. There's no law against that. You make it sound like I'm some kind of stalker."

"That sounds accurate," I said. "A stalker with a camera who makes a living by taking photos of famous people. People who happened to be eating dinner out tonight. What an exciting story." I rolled my eyes.

"Three of you with a beautiful mystery woman," Belinda said. "That could be a very exciting story." She was practically salivating.

"It's sweet that you think I'm beautiful," Chelsea

said, "But I'm no one. Just a student lucky enough to get a ride here from these guys."

In the corner of my eye, I caught Dallas twitching at her choice of words.

Don't think about riding Chelsea, I told myself. A boner would give the paparazzo something to talk about.

Belinda laughed again. "I'm sure you got a ride from them. Which one of them?" Her predatory gaze swivelled from one to the other of us, slightly frowning as she watched for any change in our expressions. Anything that might give us away.

It was Chelsea's turn to laugh. "You saw us get out of the SUV. Obviously I got a ride with all three of them." She shot Belinda a dazzling smile and stepped through the open door into the restaurant.

I gave Belinda a last look and curled my lip before stalking away. Seeing the smile melt off her face was satisfying. Good, she could find someone else to harass. Maybe I should give her Atlas' address.

"I hate parasites like her," I grumbled before a server led us to our table. I was so annoyed, I didn't even think to argue when Frost and Dallas sat on either side of Chelsea, leaving me to sit opposite. Dallas moved his chair a little closer, as though he couldn't bear to be too far away from her.

"She's just doing her job," Chelsea said. "Feeding the public's need for dirt on guys like you."

"The public should mind its own fucking business," Dallas growled.

"Yeah, they should, but they won't," I said. "Don't let it get to you. She'd like nothing more than to live rent free in your brain. People like her aren't worth it. Let's relax and enjoy ourselves, yeah?"

"Sounds good to me," Frost said.

We had a table in the corner where no one would disturb us, or overhear. As long as we didn't shout, we'd be left alone.

I loved that about places like this. If Belinda followed us in and tried to take photos, the staff would kick her out. I'd seen several escorted to the door in the past. Henrietta's was so exclusive, someone like Belinda would have to wait a year for a table. She couldn't pretend she was another customer so she could sit there and watch.

"How did you get us a table here?" Frost asked Dallas. "Even if I tell them who I am, it takes weeks to get a table."

"My sister owns the place," Dallas said. "Makes it easier to pull strings."

"Your sister is Henrietta?" Frost asked.

Dallas rolled his eyes. "Henrietta sold the place

years ago. My sister Greta runs the place now. I have a small stake in it, so they can't refuse when I want to come here and eat."

"Nice," I said approvingly. "I had no idea you were so connected in Dusk Bay."

Dallas shrugged. "It's one restaurant. It's not like I know the mayor, or whoever runs the place."

Chelsea poured herself a glass of water from the jug in the centre of the table and took a big gulp. She started coughing and her face turned pink.

"You okay?" I asked, while Dallas patted her on her back. He left his hand there even after she stopped coughing.

"I'm fine." She waved off my concern. "Just went down the wrong hole."

"Nothing worse than putting things in the wrong hole," I said with a grin.

"Some people would say there's no such thing as a wrong hole," Frost remarked. He selected his meal from the tablet the server left at the table, before passing it to me.

"There is if you choke to death," I said before choosing a steak and passing the tablet to Dallas.

"If you choke to death, you're doing it wrong," Frost said.

I chuckled. "Ain't that the truth? Speaking of

truth, let's play a game. Truth or dare. First question, who did you lose your virginity to?"

I raised my eyebrows at Frost. It was a silly game, but it always got the conversation flowing. Besides, I was curious about all of them and their backgrounds. If I was going to spend time with the other two guys, I wanted to dig deeper into who they were. And I wanted to get to know Chelsea better. What better way to do that?

"Truth," Frost said. "I was tutored by a girl in high school. For some reason, they thought I needed to understand Shakespeare and poetry." He grimaced.

"She was a real geek. She loved gaming and science fiction and all that stuff. She had a crush on me. I was desperate to get my dick wet. It was quick and messy, but it got the job done. Except she wasn't happy when I told her afterward that I didn't think about her that way." He shrugged and his gaze swivelled to Dallas.

"Truth," Dallas said with a grunt. "Some chick in high school. A group of us used to hang out. We went to a party one night. Started kissing and then we fucked. I barely remember it. She started going out with my friends after that. No hard feelings. It was just one of those things that happen." He didn't look like it was a life changing event for him.

I remembered the parties back then. They probably weren't sober. I'd had more than one quick, drunken fuck at nights like that. Hell, some mornings I had a vague memory of fucking someone, but not who. Everyone else was too drunk to fill me in. Whatever, it was nothing I lost any sleep over.

"Your turn, Chels," I said. "Truth or dare."

All of us looked over to Chelsea. Her face turned slightly pink. "I—" She looked past my shoulder. "Oh look, garlic bread."

A server placed the basket on the table, effectively ending the game. For now.

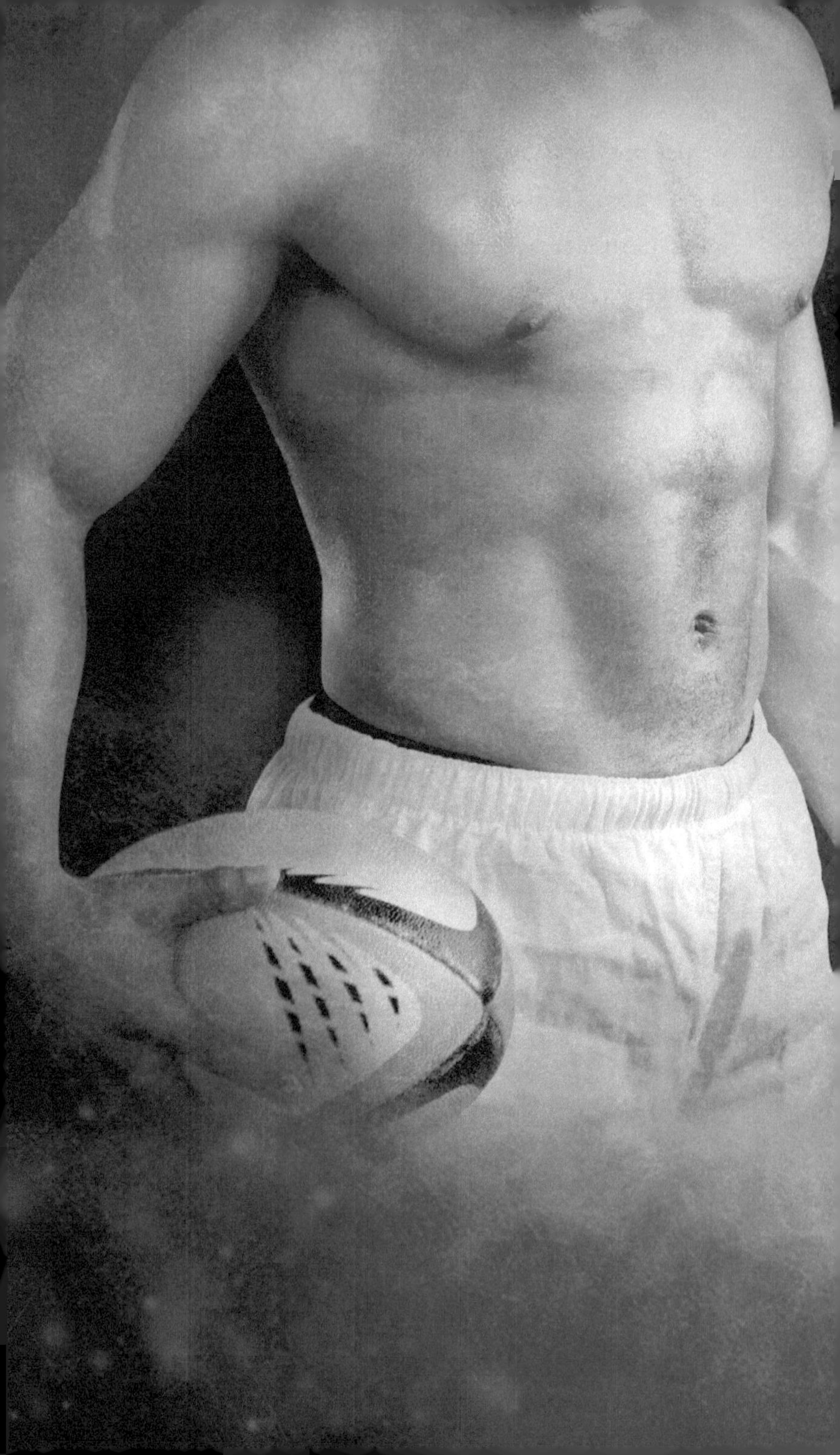

Chapter Twenty

Chelsea

The food was incredible, and the company even better. I spent most of the meal sitting back and observing while they bantered and teased each other.

At least, Storm and Frost did. Dallas spent most of the meal with a hand on my back or my thigh. He'd remove it every now and again to break apart some bread, but quickly put it back, like he couldn't bear not touching me.

"How was your ravioli?" He looked anxious, my response important to him. His stake in the restaurant must mean more to him than he initially let on.

"It was delicious," I said honestly. "I don't think I've ever had better pasta. There's nothing like freshly made."

He visibly relaxed. "Yeah, there isn't. My sister

prides herself on making everything fresh. With native ingredients and all that."

"She does a great job," Frost said. He patted his full stomach. "I'm going to have to train three times harder tomorrow. Worth it."

"Definitely," Storm agreed. He hadn't mentioned truth or dare again, but I got the impression he hadn't forgotten.

Personally, I was grateful for the garlic bread arriving when it did. He'd caught me off guard, but that wouldn't happen again. Not if I could help it.

"I should probably have insisted you all eat salad," I said. "As your doctor, I should encourage you to stick to the diet your dietician gave you."

"You're not our doctor yet," Storm pointed out. "For the record, you could have tried. I would have had the spaghetti anyway. I'll train three times harder tomorrow too."

I clicked my tongue. "Ignoring your doctor's orders." I shook my head.

No, I wasn't their doctor yet, but I soon would be. I had to be. I wouldn't let failure be an option.

"What are you going to do, spank us?" Frost asked. "Because I'd be down for that." He sipped his drink, his eyes smiled at me.

"That doesn't surprise me in the slightest," I said.

My ass was still slightly uncomfortable from the bruises Storm left behind. Not to mention the ones Dallas added.

I wouldn't say no to returning the favour with one of the guys. Or all of them. I also wouldn't object to seeing Storm leave bruises on Frost.

I saw the way they looked at each other over dinner. The occasional glance and accidental brushing of hands when they both reached for the water jug. Their connection was electric.

"How does this work?" Dallas asked, his fingers stroking the inside of my thigh. "Do we all go to someone's house, or do we take turns with Chelsea?"

"You can all come to my place," Storm said. "We can figure it out from there. Who wants to do what with whom." He propped his elbows on the table. "The rules are simple. No judgement. If anyone wants to make judgements, they can fuck off now." His gaze slid from Frost, to me, then to Dallas.

"I can agree not to judge any of you," Frost said. He turned his face and looked at Dallas.

"If you won't judge me, then I won't judge you," the second-rower said. "Another rule. No photos, no videos. No nothing that can leak to the public."

"A-fucking-men," Storm agreed. "I'd love naked photos of Chelsea, but there's too much risk of being hacked. I don't want anyone looking at her who isn't in this—" he turned his finger around in a circle, indicating everyone at the table "—whatever this is. Those days are in the past."

"Unless I decide to get naked for someone else," I said. Last time I looked, it was still my body.

"Then they better be involved in this too," Storm said firmly. "Your body is for our eyes, hands, mouths and cocks. Whether that's just us, or includes some other guys, it doesn't include the whole fucking Internet."

"Agreed," Frost said softly. "I don't want everyone seeing her either."

I could have told them I knew a couple of guys, twins, who could have anything like that taken off the Internet if I needed it. They might not be able to remove it completely, especially if people saved the photos, but they could take it down from anywhere it would be seen by a lot of people. And keep it from going back up.

I pressed my lips together instead. If I told the guys that, I'd have a lot more to explain. Stuff they might not be ready for yet.

On the drive here, I had the distinct impression they had no idea who might have followed us. That it could have been someone far worse than a paparazzo. Did they really not know who ran Dusk Bay?

If this turned into anything more than fucking, if they wanted a relationship with me, sooner or later they had to know.

I decided that was a problem for future Chelsea. I'd look for the right time to tell them, but it wasn't now.

"If anyone spreads photos of her naked, I'll poke their eyes out," Dallas growled. He picked up his fork and stabbed the air with it.

I smiled. For a big, obsessive guy, he was adorable. He'd be horrified if he knew what my brother would do. Poking people's eyes out was a relaxed Tuesday afternoon for Isaac 'Ice' Miller.

"It would be best not to take any photos, or videos," I said finally. "I wouldn't want anyone to do anything rash or violent on my behalf."

Not that would get them kicked off the team, anyway. If Dallas was going to go around stabbing anyone, he'd have to make sure they were dead and the evidence dealt with first.

Once again, I knew people.

Once again, I couldn't tell him that.

"Does that mean photos of you are fair game?" Frost asked Dallas teasingly.

Dallas aimed the fork in his direction and repeated the stabbing motion. "I have a contract. The only photos I allow to be circulated are ones that pass through my management."

"That doesn't rule out naked ones," Frost pointed out.

"If my management wants to circulate naked photos of me to boost my career, I'll let them." Dallas placed his fork on his plate. "Otherwise, not a chance."

Storm looked thoughtful.

"What is it?" I ask him.

Smiling, he said, "I was wondering what circumstances naked photos of us would boost our careers. We're supposed to be role models for children. It seems unlikely, worse luck."

"You want to pose naked?" Frost asked. "I mean, from the front."

"I wouldn't want to put all the other men on the planet to shame," Storm said. "But it wouldn't bother me. I'm not shy about my body. If I didn't play rugby, I'd make an amazing porn star." He cut a look toward Dallas. "So would you. Watching you fuck Chelsea got me going the other night. I bet you'd make a fortune."

Dallas shrugged. "Probably, but I'll stick to footy."

"You wouldn't want to make a living by fucking?" I asked.

I'd been approached a couple of times by people who made adult videos, but I'd declined. If I gave up medicine, I would have jumped at the chance, but it'd be difficult to get a job as a doctor if I was out there, on the Internet, as a porn actor.

"I'd rather make a living by tackling people into the turf," Dallas said. "Making them bleed is more satisfying."

"Right?" Storm asked. "If we weren't on the field, what we do is illegal. Or at least, something for behind closed doors." He raised his eyebrows at me and smiled.

I smiled back before turning to Dallas. "You enjoy making people bleed?" I'd barely scratched the surface of what he was into. I didn't have much experience with knives. Divina didn't allow them, and no one I'd ever been with was interested.

As for me, I'd always been curious to try.

Dallas swallowed visibly and his hand tightened on my thigh. "I guess so." He grimaced. "I'm so fucking hard now. If we don't get out of here, I'm going to take you into the kitchen and fuck you in front of the kitchen staff."

"I don't see a problem with that," Frost said.

Dallas swivelled around to look at him. "Hot oil, *dickhead*. Kitchens are dangerous. You don't fuck in, or with, kitchens." He relaxed slightly. "Not restaurant ones anyway. At home, that's a different story."

Frost held his hands up in surrender. "Okay, got it. You don't want your cock burnt off. I can respect that."

Dallas shook his head and rolled his eyes before pushing himself to his feet and taking my arm to pull me up with him. "No I don't. If that's what you're into, then go for it. I won't be here to hear you scream."

I bit my lip to keep from smiling. My brother would love this conversation. He would have been inspired. The next man in his workroom would probably have his cock burnt off, so Isaac could see what it was like.

Knowing him, he had a thousand other ideas without getting any from us.

"Hard pass," Frost said. "I like my cock not melted." He patted his groin.

"Wise decision," Storm told him.

"I thought so," Frost agreed. "Although, I think it's the *only* decision. Unless a person is really sadistic."

"I think the word you're looking for is masochistic," Storm said. "Either way, an intact cock sounds better." He patted Frost on the shoulder before heading for the door.

Dallas placed his hand on my lower back and we followed them out to the car park.

I half expected to see Belinda waiting for us, leaning against the side of her car, camera in hand. She would have had a cold couple of hours standing out here, but people do all sorts of strange, uncomfortable things for money.

Where her car was parked, a sedan now sat, popping and groaning now and again as the engine cooled. Long and dark, with tinted windows, if it was the one following us, I would have freaked out.

Nothing good ever seemed to come from being followed by dark sedans with tinted windows. Of course, lots of the cars in Dusk Bay fit that description. So much so, they barely stuck out any more. My yellow hatchback was more eye-catching than this vehicle. That was a choice I made deliberately, in the hope it would indicate I stayed out of the darker shadows of the city.

Still, seeing it made me nervous.

"Any sign of the leech?" Storm stopped and turned a slow circle, looking around the car park and out onto the street.

"She's probably long gone by now," Frost said. "Annoying the shit out of someone else."

"That's someone who needs their eyes poked out," Dallas said darkly. "I remember a few years ago, a paparazzo followed around that singer, Abbie Hart. Next thing, she was mysteriously dead."

"I remember that," I said. "Abbie was touring with Wolf Venom at the time."

I was a big fan of her and the band. Their collaborations were some of my favourite songs. I'd met most of Wolf Venom in passing, but didn't know any of them well. Well enough to know it wasn't that much of a mystery that anyone harassing their girlfriend died. All of them were very protective of her, and most had the skills, connections and experience to kill someone and make it look like an accident.

"Yeah," Dallas said. "That's a precedent I could get behind." He glared off into the darkness, as though Belinda would see him. If she could, and was as smart as I thought she was, she'd be very careful from now on. Making her disappear wouldn't be difficult.

Neither Storm nor Frost disagreed with Dallas. Even if they didn't know what Dusk Bay was really like, they seemed to have caught on to the vibe.

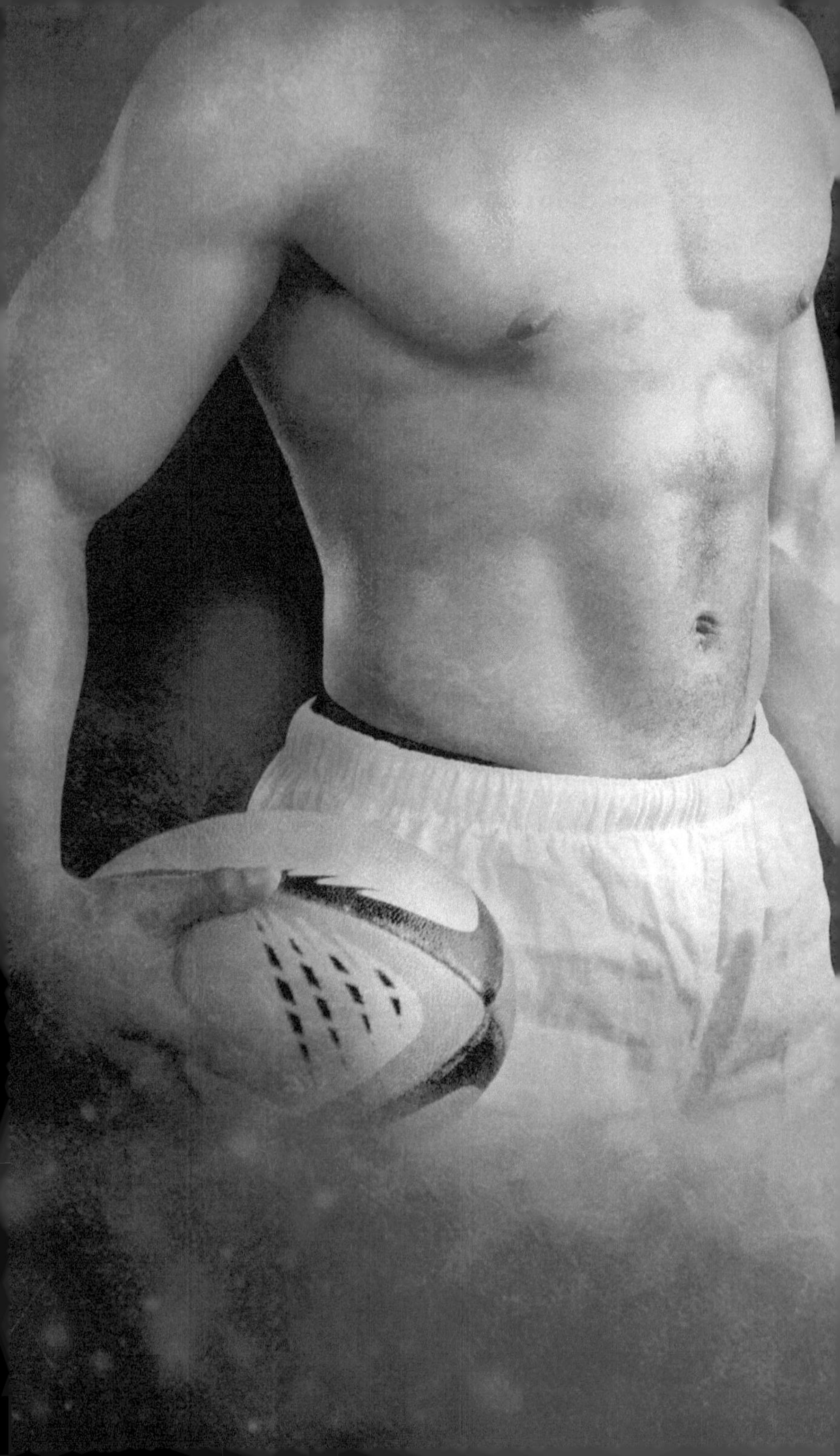

Chapter Twenty One

Chelsea

STORM BARELY CLOSED AND LOCKED THE DOOR behind us when Dallas pressed me against the wall and kissed me. His hands were up the front of my shirt, cupping my breasts, making my nipples hard. He groaned, his erection pressing into me.

His desperate need was contagious.

I gripped his firm ass, holding him closer. I needed him inside me. Right now. Too many layers of clothing lay between us.

We tugged at each other's shirts. Somehow pulled them off and tossed them aside.

I was vaguely aware of him unhooking my bra, before the cooler air hit my breasts, making my nipples harder still.

He pulled me away from the wall and turned me around.

I found my back pressed against Storm's chest, Storm's arms around me. Big hands caressed my breasts while Frost and Dallas worked off the rest of my clothes.

Storm held me in place against him while Dallas kicked off his jeans and boxers.

The second-rower gripped my ass, lifted me and wrapped my legs around his waist.

Both guys supporting my weight, I leaned back and let Dallas slide his cock into me.

Storm supported my thighs in either hand, keeping them up and open, while his teammate fucked me hard.

At the same time, Frost slipped his hand between us to massage my clit with his fingers. "Now this is what I call teamwork."

Storm snorted a laugh and kissed the side of my neck, teasing the sensitive skin there with his tongue.

I moaned softly, overwhelmed by the feeling of being touched by three men at the same time. Never for a moment did I think they might drop me. Their bodies were firm, strong and solid. With them, I felt safe. Cared for.

"Fuck," Dallas whispered. "You feel so fucking good."

"So do you," I said, meaning all of them. Frost had the perfect rhythm to tap my piercing against my clit, driving me absolutely wild. "I'm so close."

"Don't let her come too soon," Storm warned.

Frost looked at me, then at him. He took his hand off my clit and moved it to the back of Storm's neck. He pulled him over for a heated kiss.

The sight made me moan again. The clash of tongues, teeth and stubble was one of the hottest things I'd seen in a long time. Maybe ever.

"Holy hell," Dallas whispered. He was staring at them too, pausing while buried inside me.

"You want some too?" Storm asked, breaking off the kiss. "Frosty."

"My pleasure." Frost took a step or two over and pressed his mouth to Dallas'.

The second-rower seemed stunned for a moment before he started kissing him back, his tongue stroking over Frost's lower lip.

Storm nuzzled his face into me. "You like what you see?" His voice was deep and husky. His erection pressed against my ass cheek.

"Definitely." I wanted to memorise every moment, sear it into my brain.

It was over too quickly, but then Frost caressed my clit again, pushing me back to the edge of oblivion. I couldn't have stopped myself from coming if I tried. I leaned back against Storm's body and came hard around Dallas' cock. A heartbeat or two later, he followed me, coming with a moan.

"Fuck yeah. So fucking...good." He grunted and went still, spilling himself into me.

The warmth of his release flooded me, filling me.

He exhaled a long breath and sagged forward. For a couple of minutes he stayed that way, eyes closed, cock still deep inside me. He didn't move, savouring the moment and our connection. No hurry to break it until he was ready. Even then, he stayed that way before exhaling again, this time a huff of reluctance.

"I could sleep inside you." Slowly, he pulled out and he and Storm carefully lowered me to the floor.

My feet barely touched hardwood when Storm guided me over to the couch and bent me over the arm. I hadn't seen him shed his clothes, but he was naked now, his hands gripping my hips as he guided himself inside me.

"Frost, come and fuck her mouth," he order.

"Hell yeah, happy to." Frost gripped my chin

between his thumb and forefinger and turned my face so he could slide his cock between my lips.

I opened eagerly, teasing his head with the tip of my tongue and tasting the salt of his pre-cum.

"Mmm." Frost tilted his head back and his hips forward, ready to thrust when I closed my mouth over him.

"That's it." Storm drove in and out of me with even strokes, setting the pace for all of us. "Dallas, she feels even better with your cum inside her," he ground out.

Dallas stood close by, watching, his cock half-hard and glistening with our combined release. By the expression on his face, he was also memorising this moment. Savouring the sight of me being fucked by two of his teammates. He was watching them too, his gaze taking in their hard bodies.

Beyond that, what went on behind his hazel eyes was hard to read. If he wanted to touch them himself, I couldn't tell.

It was possible he didn't know either. This situation was new for all of us. They had a lot to learn about each other and themselves. Whatever conclusions they came to, I was here for it. Learning and exploring made life worth living, in my opinion.

"What do you want, Chels?" Storm asked. He'd

slowed his strokes, stopping each time he was seated all the way inside, taking a breath before pulling back out.

I drew my face back, letting Frost's cock pop out from between my lips. "I want to see you kiss again."

I wanted more, a lot more, but for now, I wanted that. Anything else would happen when the time was right. When they were ready.

"Whatever the lady wants." Storm took my arm just above my elbows and pulled out of me. He turned me around and sat me on the side of the couch, my legs wrapped around him, before pushing back in.

I hooked my ankles behind his waist, holding him close while he snaked an arm around Frost's neck and pulled him in for a scorching kiss. He thrust his tongue into Frost's mouth, in rhythm with his thrusts into me.

"So fucking hot," I whispered. Between my release, Dallas' cum and this, I was drenched. Slick with arousal. The smell of sex lingered in my nostrils, headier than any drug. If I could, I'd stop time and live in this night forever.

Eventually, and with reluctance, they pulled apart.

Storm slid his cock out of my pussy and guided me around to the other side of the couch. He lay back and lowered me down onto him, facing away from him. His hands hard enough to bruise, he gripped my arms and pulled my upper body back, opening me out wide.

Frost stood beside us. He palmed his cock a couple of times, stroking it slowly before pressing his throbbing flesh back between my lips.

At the same time, Dallas knelt beside the couch, and angled himself so his head was between my legs. He swiped his tongue up and down my pussy, teasing and tasting me.

Storm slowly thrust up into me, careful not to dislodge Dallas' mouth.

I dropped my gaze to watch Dallas. Every so often, the back of his tongue tapped Storm's cock. Both of them twitched each time, but neither made a move to pull away. If anything, they both seemed to add that to the list of moments to savour. To repeat later.

I thought being touched before by all three of them was hot, but this was something else. With one fucking my pussy, one fucking my mouth and another fucking me with his mouth, I was helpless to do anything but come again. And again.

Storm groaned and came hard under me, his thrusts still slow, but firmer.

"Chels, fucking hell woman..." he ground out. "Take...my cum." He grunted, giving me all he had, flooding me again with pearly heat.

"That's so—" Whatever it was, Frost's words were cut off a moment later, when he also came, squirting salty, cum down my throat. He groaned long and low as I sucked harder, milking him for everything he had. Wanting to make his pleasure last as long as mine. Sucking and licking until he finally sagged beside me.

Smiling, satisfied for now, he slid his cock out from between my lips.

I locked my eyes on his and swallowed every delicious drop.

Storm was barely lifting me off his cock when Dallas pulled me to the edge of the couch and impaled me again on his cock.

"He's a machine," Frost marvelled.

Dallas cut him a glance. "Can't get enough of her." He drove in hard, over and over, as though he hadn't fucked me for days. As though if he did it hard enough, he might embed himself in me, and never leave.

With a guttural groan, he came again, filling me

for a third time. He slumped over me, puffing and sweating slightly.

"We need to get her washed up," Storm said.

"And ready for round two," Frost said. "Or three, if Dallas is up to a third."

"Fucking right I'll be ready." Dallas helped me up and we walked to the bathroom, cum trickling down my thighs.

Chapter Twenty Two

Chelsea

"Three of them?" Sadie stared at me. "For real? How are you still able to walk?"

"With a bit of difficulty," I said with a laugh. "But I have no regrets. Although I was tired at work today."

Doctor Stuart kept giving me worried glances, but he didn't say anything. Presumably, he was waiting for me to ask for help if I needed it. Instead, I got on with my job. Today, that included watching the guys train. They were impressive, driven and skilled, even though they gave each other hell every chance they got. Coach Stanley and the rest of the team had their hands full with them.

"Excuse me if I don't have too much sympathy," Sadie said with a smile. "Three hot ruck boys. Phew,

Chels." She fanned herself with her hand. "Can you introduce me to some of them?"

"When are you short of attention from men?" I asked.

She was absolutely gorgeous. Wherever she went, she caught their eyes. She only had to snap her fingers and they'd come running.

"Never three at once," she argued. "You're my hero right now." She sipped her coffee while the breeze off the bay ruffled her hair.

The day was chilly, but the outdoor section of the café was the perfect place to talk without being overheard. "So, what's the plan?"

"What plan?" I poked my cheesecake with my fork.

"Do you have a future with any of them?" she pressed, as if I was deliberately being obtuse. "Are you going to settle down some day and become a rugby wife?"

"I have no idea," I said. "I'm not sure if I could pick between them. I'm not even sure they'd let me."

"Am I sensing some possessive vibes?" Her expression went from slightly envious, to slightly concerned. "Do we need an intervention? Or a new identity?"

I cocked my head at her and made a face. "No and no. It's nothing I can't handle."

"So to speak," she said with a grin. "It sounds like a lot of handling took place."

I rolled my eyes at her, but smiled. I'd told her about my date and the night at Storm's place, telling her I'd fucked all three of them several times. Beyond that, I hadn't gone into specific detail.

"You're not denying it," she pointed out. "What are they like? I bet they're huge. They look like guys who'd have big dicks."

"I'm not sure they'd appreciate me discussing their penis size," I said. They probably wouldn't care, but I wasn't going to anyway. She wasn't at Flirts on the night Dallas fucked me in front of everyone else, or she would have seen for herself. Since that part of my life was over, she was out of luck.

She pouted playfully. "How am I supposed to live vicariously through you when you won't give me the details?"

"How about you live your own life?" I suggested. "I bet you wouldn't have trouble finding three guys who wanted to have fun with you."

She shrugged. "I guess so, but would they be professional athletes?"

I caught sight of movement behind her shoulder and pressed my lips together.

"What is it?" Sadie looked over her shoulder.

"More of a who than a what," I said.

It could be a coincidence that Belinda Simmons *happened* to be in the same café as us. It was probably *not* a coincidence that she chose a table where she could see me and possibly hear what I was saying.

"Friend of yours?" Sadie turned back around.

"Definitely not," I said. I briefly told her about the paparazzo following us to the restaurant, and the conversation outside the door.

"Yuck," Sadie said. "I mean, I read those kinds of magazines, but it's not fun when they're talking about you."

"Says the woman who, moments ago, wanted to live vicariously through me," I said, my voice low.

"That's exactly my point," she replied. "I want to keep that to myself. It's one thing for me to fantasise about the things you do, but not the rest of the world." She grinned around the rim of her mug before taking a sip.

"Never say that again," I said, slightly pained. "That you fantasise about anything I do."

"Sorry, not sorry," she laughed. "I guess I'm not getting any more salacious details."

"I'm regretting saying as much as I did," I said ruefully. "But certainly not in front of her."

I nodded towards Belinda. I wanted her to know I'd seen her sit down, and wasn't happy about it. If she thought stalking me would get her anywhere, she better think again.

As if that was her cue, Belinda stood and walked over to us, her heels clicking on the concrete. Her hips swung like she wanted everyone to notice her.

"How nice to see you again," she gushed, her smile as fake as fuck. "How was your dinner the other night? I hear Henrietta's is exceptional."

"It was fine," I said. I returned her fake smile. We both knew she may never find out what the food there was like. That was definitely not my problem. If I was petty, I'd be happy she was missing out.

She gave me a dismissive wave of her hand. "I'm sure it was more than fine. Especially with such fascinating company." She leaned down, palms on the table top, displaying her cleavage. "If you wanted to talk to me about them, I could make it worth your while."

"Thank you, but I'm not interested in women," I

said, pretending to misunderstand. "And if I was, my friend here would be first in line."

"I would?" Sadie sat up taller and grinned like a kid who was offered a gold star. "I mean, of course I would, I'm amazing." She pretended to fluff her red hair. She was no more interested in me that way than I was in her, but neither of us could resist trying to get a rise out of the paparazzo.

Belinda scowled at her obvious sarcasm and my, also obvious, attempt to be obtuse. She straightened up and crossed her arms under her breasts. "I was referring to money. I don't need to resort to sex in order to do my job."

Was she trying to imply that I did? The desire to scratch her eyes out was becoming stronger.

Sadie laughed. "I bet you do. Or at least, I bet you would if you could get a story that would make you millions. Who wouldn't? Sometimes a girl has to do what a girl has to do, right Chels?"

I winced. Until now, Belinda didn't know my name. Now she did, it might be that much easier for her to figure out exactly who I was.

"I'm sure Melinda wouldn't do anything like that," I said, pretending I couldn't remember her name.

"Belinda," she said from behind clenched teeth. "Of course I wouldn't, thank you Chels."

Sadie winced, realising her mistake too late. "So anyway, unless you wanted something, we were having a private conversation. Sooo sorry." She smirked.

Belinda smirked back and returned her attention to me. "Think about it. One story that captures the public interest could make us both a lot of money. You could become famous."

"I don't want to be famous," I said. "That's actually the point. That and, if I had anything juicy on any of them, I wouldn't tell you. You can come sniffing around all you like, but you won't find anything here."

"See..." She drew out the word. "I don't believe you. I know a good story when I see one and you, dear, are it."

"Are you old enough to call her dear?" Sadie squinted at Belinda. "Next thing, you'll be calling her pet."

I grimaced. "I'm no one's pet." Although, doggy style was one of my favourite positions. And Storm's.

"Of course you're not." Sadie leaned over to pat my hand. I thought she might make a pussy joke, but for once she didn't. Knowing her, she'd hold onto it until after Belinda was gone. If she'd leave us alone.

"Which one of them are you sleeping with?" Belinda asked, obviously trying to take me by surprise.

Since it was such an obvious question, I was ready for it. Even if I wasn't, I'd fielded questions like that for the last couple of years, as a dancer at Flirts. New customers always wanted to ask about the famous ones, they couldn't seem to help themselves. They wanted to be the guy who fucked the woman who fucked an Oscar winner. It was a strange ambition, but here we were.

"Who says I'm sleeping with one of them?" I asked sweetly. Not much sleep happened, but all three of them were involved, not just one.

"My journalist senses," Belinda said. "Like I said, I can see a story from a mile away. Why wouldn't you be sleeping with an attractive, single rugby player?"

"I think you're projecting," Sadie said. "How many rugby players have rejected your advances?"

Belinda ignored her.

"I know this is wild," I said slowly. "But it's possible for men and women to interact without sex involved."

Okay, I felt like a massive hypocrite for saying

that. So much of my life revolved around sex. It had for a long time. But it was also true that I'd interacted with lots of men and we hadn't touched, much less anything else.

"I know it's possible," Belinda said. "But in this case, I know you're sleeping with one of them. "If you just tell me—"

"Hell would freeze over before I told you anything like that," I snapped. She was pushing me to the edge of my last nerve, and she was doing it on purpose. I knew that, but I couldn't seem to contain my irritation any longer. She was trying to get me to reveal something out of frustration, or anger.

She smiled. The kind of look that suggested I'd confided all my secrets to her. "That was what I thought."

"I'm surprised you're capable of thinking," Sadie muttered.

"Whatever you think you know—" I started.

"You'll read about it in the morning," she said. "Thank you, this has been very informative. It's a shame you didn't want to share in the money I'll be making from this." She looked incredibly smug. Nodding to me, then to Sadie, she backed away and left.

"She's bluffing," Sadie said. "She can't possibly have learnt anything from what you said."

I picked up my spoon and stabbed it into the cheesecake, leaving it standing vertically. "She might not be, but maybe she picked up on something I said accidentally. People like her are—"

"Full of shit," Sadie finished for me. "If she says anything about you, it'll be made up. Then you can make a lot of money by suing her ass."

Or she might publish something that made me lose my job.

Chapter Twenty Three

Storm

Teeth clenched around my mouthguard, I ran a couple of steps and lunged. The winger tried to swerve, but I came at him from an angle, grabbing him in a side tackle and bringing us both down to the ground. The ball slipped out of his grasp and went flying. It was snatched up by the eight man and passed back, down the field.

I rolled over and jumped back to my feet, my concentration not lapsed for a moment.

I lived for days like these. Days when there was nothing else on my mind but the game I loved. Nothing and no one else existed for now. Just the rush of blood through my ears and the men around me.

All I needed was an audience and I'd be in my element.

Willy Jones, known to most of us as Free Willy, caught the ball and bolted, slamming it and himself down beyond the try line, landing clear of the offence's attempted ankle tap.

The coach blew the whistle, calling an end to the training session.

I grunted with annoyance.

When I was in the zone, I hated having to snap out of it. The adrenaline was still thumping through me. It always took time to work its way through my system and out. I didn't want it to. I liked the rush it gave me. It was better than skydiving. Better than anything but sex.

"Hey." Frost walked alongside me, towards the locker rooms. "We've hit form right on time."

I glanced over at him before pulling out my mouthguard and shaking off the saliva.

"There's always room for improvement. We can do better than we are. Sloppy ball handling and tackles. Communication." I shrugged. Too many times, guys missed opportunities they shouldn't. During a game, the opposition would take full advantage. We'd be creamed. Not in the good way.

"I guess," Frost said in a way that suggested he

wasn't paying complete attention to my gripe. Usually he agreed with me.

I glanced over to him. "What's up? Regrets?"

"No," he said quickly. "The opposite. It's weird to talk about, you know?"

"Yeah, big scary feelings," I said, only half-sarcastic. I wasn't good at talking about those either. Even if those feelings were only arousal. I was in no way ready to talk about relationships or shit like that. We were friends who fucked the same woman, and had kissed. That was all I could get my head around for now.

His jaw tensed. "If that's all you're going to—"

I stopped and punched him on the arm. "I'm not making fun. It was good. Let's do it again. Okay?"

He stared at me for a while before his jaw relaxed again. "Okay."

We resumed walking, falling silent for a few moments.

"You're wondering what else?" I asked, continuing to keep it deliberately vague. Dallas was a few metres away, but we were surrounded by a group of other players, including Atlas and Jay. "I don't know what else."

I caught the look of disappointment on his face and added, "For now. You're usually the one who jumps into things, not me. Don't ask me to decide on something just like that."

"Right." He stepped into the locker room first and sat down to pull off his boots.

I sat down beside him. "That wasn't what you wanted to hear."

He shrugged. "I get it. One day at a time."

"Exactly," I agreed. "I'm not ruling anything out." I leaned over, hands on my lace, paused in the middle of untying it. "Like you said, it's weird to talk about."

'I want to fuck you' weren't words I'd ever said to another man. Thought them? Yes. But where I came from, saying things like that out loud could get you beaten to a pulp. For broaching the subject at all, he was braver than me. His childhood wasn't that different from mine. Small towns and small minds. Nothing better to do than gossip and judge, and raise fists against people who made you uncomfortable. Assholes.

"When you're ready to talk about it, I'm here." He glanced over at me and offered the faintest smile. One that sent a sliver of heat right to my balls, and threatened to make cracks in my armour.

I couldn't and wouldn't act on that, not here, not today. Part of me hated myself for it. As my father used to say, I was old enough and ugly enough to make my own decisions. I shouldn't be letting other people's bullshit make them for me.

All I could say in response was, "Yeah."

Fucking coward, I told myself.

"You guys good?" Dallas sat on the other side of Frost.

"Peachy," Frost said, forcing a smile. "Ready for the season opener."

Dallas nodded, but clearly knew that wasn't what we were talking about. "We'll kill this season."

"And if we don't, Chelsea will be there to kiss us better," Frost said.

Dallas' eyes immediately darkened at the mention of her.

I thought she was getting under my skin, but it was nothing compared to his reaction to her. He was obsessed with her. Borderline addicted. Hell, maybe not even borderline. I'd seen him out on the paddock, struggling to focus on the game. By the end of the training session, he had his head in the right place, but if he was going to do that during an actual game, we could be in trouble.

I had no idea what the solution to that was. He wasn't going to stop seeing her and the team needed him to play.

The deeper we all got, the more complicated this became. I didn't regret a single second. I hoped he doesn't give me a reason to.

"Who are you guys talking about?" Atlas stopped in front of us, his customary smirk in place. With his light brown curls and brown eyes with stupidly long lashes, some people might call him attractive. His looks were evenly balanced by being an asshole.

"You," I shot back. "If any of us are hurt, you'll be there to kiss us better, right?" I made kissing sounds at him.

His smirk became a curled lip of disgust. "Fuck off, Keller. I wouldn't kiss you if you were the last person on the face of the planet."

"If I was the last person on the face of the planet, you wouldn't be around to kiss me," I reasoned. "We'd have to be the two last people on the planet." I gave him a smug smile.

"You're an idiot," he said. "You know what I meant."

"Did I?" I said with mock innocence. I turned sideways and glanced at Frost. "Did you know what he meant?"

"I did, but I like your answer better," Frost said. "I mean, you're not technically incorrect."

I looked back at Atlas and nodded. "There it is. I'm not wrong."

"Neither am I," Atlas said. "You're still an idiot. Who's Chelsea, and does she need me to recommend a good ophthalmologist? If she'd want to kiss any of you, she clearly needs her eyesight tested."

"You're giving me a headache with your big words." I rubbed my temples. "Did you eat a thesaurus?"

"No, I got an education," he retorted. "Something the Sydney Devils appreciate."

"You're not a Devil anymore," Frost said. "Maybe they didn't appreciate it enough."

The look Atlas gave him could have bored a hole right through his forehead.

"He shoots, he scores," I said. I offered Frost a fist bump.

"Maybe you should lay off," Dallas said softly. "Changing teams is hard enough without you guys being pricks about it."

We all gave him a surprised look.

He shrugged at us. "Just saying."

"I don't need them to be nice," Atlas said. "Tell Chelsea I said hi." He turned and walked away.

I resisted the urge to jump to my socked feet and strangle the living shit out of him. If he so much as looked at her the wrong way, I might give in to that urge.

Maybe I should, because sooner or later he'd meet her and that occurrence wasn't without the risk that he'd get sucked into her orbit too. I'd rather face an hour-long session talking about my deepest feelings than consider sharing her with him as well.

"Sometimes, I think it might be better if she didn't end up working here," Frost said slowly. Reluctantly.

Now it was him I stared at. "What are you talking about?"

"Same question," Dallas snapped. "You know that's what she wants." And what he wanted, too. I'd seen him once or twice sneak off for a while and come back looking more satisfied than he had when he left. It doesn't take a genius to work out what he was doing and who he was doing it with. At no time was I jealous; I'd have my time with her later.

"First of all, you might get your shit together better if she wasn't so close," Frost said to Dallas. "And none of the other guys would get to meet her if she wasn't here."

"They'd meet her sooner or later," I said. "We hang out with some of them, sometimes."

"Yes, but we get to choose who we hang out

with," Frost said. "If we don't invite guys like him, they won't see her in person."

"We'd need to ban her from coming to any of our games," I said, slowly cottoning on to what he was saying. "Or make sure she sits where they can't see her."

"You guys are out of your minds," Dallas snarled, while still keeping his voice down. "You can't keep her from her job. She'll be furious."

"She has another job she can go back to," I said. I didn't like that option either. I preferred it when we weren't sharing her with the gazes of other men.

"No way," Frost said immediately. "That's out."

"I agree," Dallas said, still glowering. "Come up with another solution." He pushed himself to his feet and stomped away.

"We will," I said to his back. Even if I had to strangle Atlas for real, I'd keep him from her.

"We'll figure it out," Frost said.

I worked my jaw back and forth a couple of times. "Yeah. We have to. I'm not letting anyone fuck this up for us."

"What are you going to do if Atlas decides he likes me?" Frost asked teasingly.

That was an easy answer. "I'll rip his nuts off and feed them to him."

"I'm touched." Frost grinned.

I gave him a long look. Not yet he wasn't, but that might change soon.

"I'm hitting the showers." I tugged off my socks and stood. I had some thinking to do and a date to plan. Something that would bind Chelsea to me forever, mind, body and heart. Not to mention her wrists, preferably to my bed. Maybe I should leave her there. That would solve most of my problems.

Now my balls ached. I might have to pay a visit to the infirmary. For medical reasons, of course.

Chapter Twenty Four

Chelsea

I was no assassin, but I could move quietly when I wanted to.

Right now, there wasn't much need. The target of my visit was hunched over a keyboard, headphones over her ears. Every so often, she'd groove to whatever she was listening to. Her attention was on the music and the screen in front of her.

I stood watching her for a while, until she gradually became aware of my presence.

Belinda sat upright before swivelling around in her chair. Her eyes widened. She pulled off the headphones and tossed them onto the keyboard.

"How did you get in here?" she demanded.

I shrugged one shoulder, keeping the gun in my other hand still. "I broke in. It wasn't difficult. You should have better security if you don't want visitors."

She glanced down at the gun, then back up at me again. She seemed certain I wouldn't use it. That was a mistake. In Dusk Bay, arrogance got you killed.

"It wasn't difficult to find you once I knew your name." She sat back in her chair and crossed her arms.

She'd changed out of her skirt and blouse, and now wore fleecy pyjamas. Her hair was in a messy bun. It made her look younger, more human. If it wasn't for the expression on her face, I might have given her some leniency. As it was, I let her keep talking.

"Chelsea Miller," she said, without looking back at the screen. "Doctor." She moved her head back and forth like a bobble head, as if somehow I was showing off with the qualification.

"Employed at Flirts, adult entertainment club. Stripper, hooker, or both?"

"Both," I said unapologetically. "Former employee. I no longer work at that particular establishment."

Without unfolding her arms, she waved a hand dismissively. "A minor detail. The public will love to hear that three of the Smashers were in the company of a prostitute. One that is also passing herself off as a candidate for team doctor. A very juicy story, wouldn't you say?"

"Not really," I said. "It seems kinda boring to me. Since I am an actual qualified doctor and a suitable candidate for team doctor, the whole thing has a bunch of holes in it."

She snorted. "I'm sure you'd like to believe that, but we'll let the public decide. Your timing is perfect; I was just about to upload my article."

"No you weren't," I said evenly. "You're going to delete it and forget everything you think you know."

"Why would I do that?" she asked with a laugh. "I'm about to break the story of the year. This is going to go global and make me a ton of money." She was practically rubbing her hands together and counting her millions.

"In case you hadn't noticed, I have a gun in my hand, aimed at you," I said. I waved a hand over the top of the barrel.

"You're not going to use that," she scoffed. "Aren't doctors supposed to protect people and keep them alive?"

I smiled. "Who said anything about killing you? To be perfectly honest, I'd prefer not to. It's messy and makes complications I don't have time for. Do us both a favour and delete the article. Forget you ever saw me and move on to some other bullshit. Write something useful, like an article on how to prevent ingrown toenails. Plenty of people could use that information."

"You're out of your mind." Her chin was raised, but for the first time she looked uncertain.

"You clearly haven't had an ingrown toenail," I said, wincing melodramatically. "They fucking hurt. You'd be doing the community an important service. You'd save so many people so much pain." I wasn't even joking. I had one in high school and it sucked.

"That's not the kind of journalism I do, dear," she said, condescension back in place. "I dig deep and uncover scandals like yours. People should know the players they look up to, players who are supposed to be role models, are eliciting the services of prostitutes. All three of them are bringing the team into disrepute by being in your company."

"The company of a team doctor?" I shook my head. "How awful."

Unfortunately, she wasn't wrong. The moment people found out what I used to do, I'd be condemned. The team would have no choice but to cut me loose. The guys might hold on to their contracts, but I'd be dragged all the way through the mud. I'd be the scapegoat in the story.

No doubt the Smashers' PR department would spin it to make it look like the guys had no idea. By the time they were done, my reputation would be completely destroyed.

No way was I going to let that happen. I'd do whatever it took to stop it.

"I see you finally understand the situation you're in," Belinda said gleefully. "Add in a bit of breaking and entering and pointing a gun at me. Is that even real? And you, dear, will be in a lot of trouble."

"This is your last chance," I said as pleasantly as I could. I was tempted to kill her for continuing to call me dear. It was beyond annoying. "Delete the article and walk away."

She shook her head at me and turned back to the keyboard. "All I need to do is press enter, and it'll be uploaded for all the world to see."

Her finger hovered over the enter button. She lowered the pad of her pointer finger to the plastic.

I raised the gun and pulled the trigger.

Thanks for reading! The story continues in Hard Ruck.

For a bonus scene of Storm giving Chelsea a bath, you can find that here.

If you haven't met her brother Isaac, also known as Ice, you can find him in Dark Masque. Rest assured he will be getting cameos in later books of the Ruck Boys series!

About the Author

Maggie Alabaster writes reverse harem romance.

She lives in NSW, Australia with one spouse, two daughters, one dog, and countless birds.

Sign up for Maggie's newsletter! Sign Up!

Join Maggie's reader group! Join here!

Follow Maggie on Bookbub! Click here to follow me!

Check out Maggie's website- www.maggiealabaster.com

Also by Maggie Alabaster

Ruck Boys

Filthy Ruck

Hard Ruck

Twisted Ruck

Sparrow and the Mafia Kings

Possessive

Ruined

Corrupted

Pucking Dark Hearts

Pucking Hearts Collide

Pucking Forbidden Hearts

Pucking Hardened Hearts

Dusk Bay Demons

Puck Drop

Breakaway

Power Play

Brutal Academy

Book 1 Heartless

Book 2 Cruel

Book 3 Vengeful

Court of Blood and Binding

Book 1 Song of Scent and Magic

Book 2 Crown of Mist and Heat

Book 3 Sword of Balm and Shadow

Book 4 Whisper of Frost and Flame

Dark Masque

Book 1 Bait

Book 2 Prey

Book 3 Trap

Saving Abbie

Book 1 Pitch

Book 2 Pound

Book 3 Session

Book 4 Muse

Book 5 Rhythm

Book 6 Encore

Novella Venomous

Saving Abbie books 1-4

Saving Abbie books 4-6 + Venomous

Ruthless Claws

Book 1 Ivory

Book 2 Crimson

Book 3 Elodie

Harmony's Magic

Book 1 Summoned by Fire

Book 2 Summoned by Fate

Book 3 Summoned by Desire

Shifter's Vault

Book 1 Discarded

Book 2 Deceived

Book 3 Disgraced

My Alien Mates

Book 1 Star Warriors

Book 2 Star Defenders

Book 3 Star Protectors

Academy of Modern Magic

Book 1 Digital Magic

Book 2 Virtual Magic

Book 3 Logical Magic

Complete Collection

Summer's Harem

Book 1: Shimmer

Book 2: Glimmer

Book 3: Flicker

Complete collection

Short reads

Taken by the Snowmen

Jingle All the Way

Also by Maggie Alabaster and Erin Yoshikawa

Caught by the Tide

Book 1—Pursued by Shadows

Book 2 Pursued by Darkness

Book 3 Pursued by Monsters

www.ingramcontent.com/pod-product-compliance
Lightning Source LLC
Chambersburg PA
CBHW030806210726

48290CB00002B/448